LAST WORDS of the HOLY GHOST

Previous Winners of the Katherine Anne Porter Prize
in Short Fiction
Laura Kopchick, series editor
Barbara Rodman, founding editor

The Stuntman's Daughter by Alice Blanchard
Rick DeMarinis, Judge

Here Comes the Roar by Dave Shaw
Marly Swick, Judge

Let's Do by Rebecca Meacham
Jonis Agee, Judge

What Are You Afraid Of? by Michael Hyde
Sharon Oard Warner, Judge

Body Language by Kelly Magee
Dan Chaon, Judge

Wonderful Girl by Aimee La Brie
Bill Roorbach, Judge

Last Known Position by James Mathews
Tom Franklin, Judge

Irish Girl by Tim Johnston
Janet Peery, Judge

A Bright Soothing Noise by Peter Brown
Josip Novakovich, Judge

Out of Time by Geoff Schmidt
Ben Marcus, Judge

Venus in the Afternoon by Tehila Lieberman
Miroslav Penkov, Judge

In These Times the Home Is a Tired Place by Jessica Hollander
Katherine Dunn, Judge

The Year of Perfect Happiness by Becky Adnot-Haynes
Matt Bell, Judge

LAST WORDS *of the* HOLY GHOST

MATT CASHION

2015 WINNER, KATHERINE ANNE PORTER PRIZE IN SHORT FICTION

University of North Texas Press
Denton, Texas

10 9 8 7 6 5 4 3 2 1

Permissions:
University of North Texas Press
1155 Union Circle #311336
Denton, Texas 76203-5017

∞The paper used in this book meets the minimum requirements of the American National Standard for Permanence of Paper for Printed Library Materials, z39.48.1984. Binding materials have been chosen for durability.

Library of Congress Cataloging-in-Publication Data

Cashion, Matthew Deshe, author.
  [Short stories. Selections]
  Last words of the Holy Ghost / by Matt Cashion.—First edition.
     p. cm.—(Number 14 in the Katherine Anne Porter Prize in Short Fiction series)
  ISBN 978-1-57441-612-1 (pbk. : alk. paper)—ISBN 978-1-57441-623-7 (ebook)
  1. Teenage boys—Southern States—Fiction. 2. Teenagers and adults—Southern States—Fiction. 3. Man-woman relationships—Southern States—Fiction. I. Title. II. Series: Katherine Anne Porter Prize in Short Fiction series ; no. 14.
  PS3603.A866A6 2015
  813'.6—dc23
                        2015024783

Last Words of the Holy Ghost is Number 14 in the Katherine Anne Porter Prize in Short Fiction Series

The electronic edition of this book was made possible by the support of the Vick Family Foundation.

Cover and text design by Rose Design

Dedication
Heather

"Doctor, if I put this here guitar down,
I ain't never gonna wake up."

> —*last words of Huddie William "Leadbelly" Ledbetter, blues musician.*

"Go away. I'm all right."

> —*last words of H.G. Wells*

Contents

The Girl Who Drowned at School That Time

Reverend Baker opened the meeting with a prayer. When he finished, everyone said *amen* and looked toward John Hampton, who took a moment to express the school board's collective grief. Hampton assured the crowd that the teacher who had failed to account for Dotty Kirkland had been suspended, pending an investigation. He then introduced the board's first order of business: to devise a strategy that would prevent other children from drowning in the school pond. Cecil Goodbread suggested the pond be drained and filled with dirt. Hampton turned Goodbread's suggestion into a motion that was seconded by Reverend Baker and approved unanimously with the sound of *aye*.

A man in a Bulldogs cap stood in the middle of the room and asked what they planned to do with all the fish, and if they didn't have any objections, could he go ahead and catch them. A man in a Gators cap asked why *that* man should be entitled to all the fish. Voices rose around the room. Hampton banged his gavel and asked for order. Goodbread declared that because the fish resided in a pond located on school grounds, the fish were considered school property and anyone caught poaching would be subject to criminal charges of trespassing. Someone claimed that Cecil just wanted the fish for himself. Cecil denied the charge. He said, "I've already *got* a freezer full of fish."

John Hampton said the issue currently residing on the table seemed to be a question of how to dispose fairly and equitably of the fish. Reverend Baker said, "Fry them." A fish-fry, he said, could be used as a revenue generator toward the purchase of new blocking dummies for the high school football team. Roosevelt Powell said what about new band uniforms? Alice Davenport wanted new landscaping. John Hampton said *Robert's Rules of Order* specified the need to vote on one motion before proceeding to the next. He said the board should hold off on deciding how to spend the revenue until they knew how much revenue the fish-fry raised, if in fact the fish-fry was something someone was going to make a motion toward.

In the form of a new motion, Rev. Baker proposed that a fish-fry be held as a revenue-generating method to dispose fairly of the fish. Cecil Goodbread seconded the motion and it was approved unanimously with the sound of *aye*. Hampton suggested the first Saturday in June so it could also serve as a function to celebrate another year of good work. He said he was sure Ms. Haven would be happy to organize the day's events. Then he moved to old business.

I never agreed to organize the fish-fry. I was sitting behind John Hampton, recording minutes, and even though I objected strongly, I did not record my objection. I saw a version of myself rise from my seat and walk from the room and down the hall and out of the building into my car and drive as far away from Dunbar Creek as I could get—away from the heat and the cruelty and the mosquitoes and the ignorance and all the good old boys whose network I helped maintain. But it was just a version of myself, and I was still very much there, weighed down by all the history in the room.

When the meeting adjourned, I typed up the minutes so John Hampton could see a copy first thing in the morning. He liked to review the language and suggest revisions.

In addition to being the minute-taker at school-board meetings, I was the Chief Administrative Assistant to the principal of Dunbar Creek Elementary School. Captain Manning, the principal, called me his secretary, because that's what he'd called Hattie Flowers, the woman who worked for forty years at the same desk I took over eight months ago. He'd hired me three minutes into my first interview without asking a single question. He ate a doughnut and sucked his fingers. A stuffed bass hung on his wall beneath a plastic fish that sang "Take Me to the River," when he pressed a button. My first job was to install new batteries.

"You can call me Captain," he said during my interview. "That's my first name and not a nickname, after my great-great-great-grandfather who served as an officer under Stonewall Jackson. He named his son Captain, and he named his son Captain, and so on, until my father named me Captain. That's him, there." He pointed to a photograph of a man holding a musket.

"I see the resemblance," I said.

"That's the Manning jaw line." He looked at the picture again and smiled. "I named my son after him too."

I scheduled his tee times and made excuses for his absences. I officiated squabbles between teachers fighting over parking spaces and copy machines. Mr. Manning told me to write upbeat affirmations on bright poster paper and hang the posters in the halls. For example: "Attitudes are contagious. Is yours worth catching?" Every day I thought of quitting, and every day I failed to quit.

The children called me Jo. They brought me candy in the mornings and asked how I was doing. The children and the candy were what got me through the days. I had my favorites. Dorothy Kirkland had been one of them. She was a strange and beautiful child with long red hair and hazel eyes, and I never saw her speak to anyone but me. She asked me once if I could come live with her, and when I laughed, she started to cry, so I said we'd be best friends instead.

I had other favorites. Christie Skelton was a shy and sickly third grader who stood outside my door before first bell, seeming to ask permission, and I'd wave her in. Sometimes she handed me a brush and turned her back to me. While I worked through her knotted hair, she told me about her family. Her sister had been killed by a twelve-year-old hunter who mistook her for a deer because she and her boyfriend, both naked, had been rolling next to some bushes at the edge of a field. Christie's father was in prison for nearly beating to death the father of the boy who'd killed his daughter. Her mother worked graveyard at the slaughterhouse, drank beer while Christie ate her cereal. Christie's grandmother lived with them too, but she never left her bed. Sometimes, Christie asked me questions.

"Jo?" she'd say.

"Yes, Christie?"

"How come you can't be my teacher instead of Mr. Cowen?"

I told her because I didn't have my certificate and therefore wasn't qualified.

She assured me that I was.

"Jo?"

"Yes, Christie?"

"Do you think I'm pretty?"

I assured her that she was.

During the first week of May, John Hampton called to ask how the fish-fry planning was coming along. I confessed that I hadn't started.

He said, "Ms. Haven—the secret to this project is delegation." Then he dictated how I should delegate. "You need to find someone who has access to water pumps and who will oversee the draining of the pond to about knee-level, then you'll need to find a group of men to walk a long seine net across the pond to herd the fish toward another group of men who will scoop them out with bare hands and nets and toss them to another group of men who will club them dead and toss them to the scalers and skinners and gutters, who will scale and skin and gut and give them to the cooks, who will roll them in flour and corn meal and drop them into gas-heated deep fryers where, once fried, they can be removed and placed in pairs inside styrofoam containers containing coleslaw and grits and hushpuppies that can then be sold for $6.95, including tea."

He asked if there were questions, though his voice told me there shouldn't be. I stared out the window toward the road and dreamed again of leaving.

My parents were waiting for me to marry, have children, dig deeper roots into Dunbar Creek. I'd come home from the state college the year before owing twenty thousand dollars in student loans. I hadn't wanted to go home. If I went home, I feared I'd get stuck, maybe married, and never leave again. I nearly went to Vietnam to teach English, and I would have, except my asshole father said if I went there not to come back, which would've been fine, except I didn't want my mother to suffer him alone. I was her only daughter. I thought she needed me.

My parents met at the chicken plant. My father's job was to rip the guts from chickens and pass the chickens to my mother, who washed them clean. They came home in bloody white coats, and throughout my early youth I pretended they were doctors. The smells sank into the carpet and drifted down the hall and covered me like an extra blanket on my bed. I tried to work at the slaughterhouse the last summer I was home from college, but I vomited every day, and my supervisor said, "We simply can't have this. You're causing unsanitary conditions."

My father asked me once a week if I was dating anyone, and once a week I told him no. When my mother held other women's grandchildren, looks of longing wet her eyes, and she looked at me so I'd be sure to notice.

All the men of Dunbar Creek, like their fathers, would die in Dunbar Creek. I was interested in none of them. I wanted to meet someone I could leave with. But no one was leaving, so I refused every invitation, even though it'd been a full year since I'd been touched. A full year since a college boyfriend left for Vietnam.

Ray, the school exterminator, was the only man I talked to regularly. He asked me out every week for eight months, and for eight months I told him no. He kept coming up with new reasons why we should get together. He said he should spray my duplex for insects. Then he wanted to show me his new truck, and then his new double-wide, and finally, his mother. He blasted through my door every Monday morning, impersonating Fats Domino: *Hello Josephine. How do you do? Do you remember me baby, like I remember you?*

He wore a green apron and a denim cap, and he kept the wallet in his back pocket fastened to his belt by a drooping chain. Ray knew nothing of the world, but he was the kindest man around. He never said any mean-spirited thing about anyone, and if someone tried to engage him in gossip, he simply shook it off. He never made one single reference, even with his eyes, that I was a little heavier than most. He was about ten years older than me, and already had some wrinkles around his eyes that made him seem wise. And when he sang his silly song, goose bumps danced up my thighs. He sprayed a lot more insecticide than he needed to, so he'd have more time to talk. He talked all the time. He even talked to me of roaches.

He'd say, "Josephine, the North American Cockroach will be the last living organism on Earth."

And I'd say, "You've told me that before, Ray."

And he'd say, "It's because their immune system continues to evolve."

Then he'd turn toward a corner and spray his insecticides, singing softly the same old song: *You used to live over yonder, by the railroad tracks. When it rained you couldn't walk. I used to tote you on my back.*

The children trusted me. Calvin Jones, a first grader, came to my office one April morning, holding both hands behind his back. He walked around my desk, saying he wanted to practice the show and tell he was supposed to perform later in the day, and when he got close enough he dropped a large hunting knife in my lap. I picked up the knife, put it in my purse and put the purse beneath my desk. Calvin put his hands on his hips and stuck out his bottom lip.

He said, "I'm telling."

"You'll get in trouble, Calvin. Captain Manning will have you sent away."

He said, "Captain Manning's a dickhead."

"Where did you get a big knife like that?"

"It's the knife my Daddy stabbed my Mama with."

"When did this happen?"

"About a few years ago."

"Is your Mama okay?"

"She dead."

"Where's your Daddy?"

"Jail."

"Who do you live with?"

"My aunt. And my cousins."

"What's your aunt do?"

"Watch TV."

I would have hugged Calvin right then, except we had a no-hugging policy at Dunbar Creek. This is what Captain Manning told me after he saw me hugging Christie Skelton one morning before school. She had come to me, saying some older boys had been touching her in the back of the bus. She was biting her bottom lip, staring at the carpet in a daze, holding her Charlie Brown lunch box with just her pinky finger. I'd only just put my arms around her when Captain Manning came through his door and summoned me to his office to tell me about the no-hugging rule, enacted by our school board attorney, who said such contact could be misconstrued as sexual harassment and thereby posed litigation risks. He recommended this after Burton Lewis, a P.E. teacher, had been accused of hugging too many of his students.

I told Captain Manning what Christie had told me about the boys on the bus. He said we had no business intervening. Government intervened in too many lives as it was, he said. The cheeks on his fat face turned red. His fat red cheeks had begun to shake.

During the final week of the school year, Ray put a penny on my desk and asked what I was thinking. He sat in the chair beside my desk and removed his hat.

He said, "You looking plumb pitiful, Josephine. Tell Uncle Ray what's got you down."

I told him I'd made no progress organizing the fish-fry and that I had no desire to start, though advertisements were already in the paper and flyers were posted all over town.

Ray said, "I'm sorry. I know you and that girl was close." He waited to see if I wanted to keep talking, but I didn't want to just then.

He slapped my desk. He said, "Tell you what. If it's okay with you, I'll make a few calls and get the whole thing taken care of. All you have to do is come to my place so I can fix you dinner."

What would one dinner hurt? I was relieved.

On the last day of the school year, Lou Duncan brought a dead squirrel to school in his lunch box and showed it to Christie, who came running to my office. I tried to get her to tell me what was wrong, but she wouldn't speak. She slumped in the chair beside my desk and stared at the floor. Becky Whittaker came into the office a little later and explained that Lou Duncan had been in the cafeteria playing "trade my lunch for your lunch" and he couldn't get any takers except for Christie, the last girl he tried, who only had an apple, which Becky had given her from her own lunch, and then Lou slid his lunch box in front of Christie and made her open it and there was this dead squirrel inside whose head was smashed and bloody and his eyes were still open and his two front teeth were hanging out over his bottom lip. I left Christie in my office and went to the cafeteria to find Lou Duncan. He was at a table with a group of boys who had the dead squirrel stretched out on the table in front of them, poking it between its hind legs with a plastic fork. I grabbed the squirrel by its tail and threw it in an outside trashcan, and little Lou Duncan followed me, saying there were plenty more where that came from.

Then Alex Hernandez and Franklin Harris got into a fist-fight in the cafeteria, which proceeded down the hall and onto the playground. They were sent to the office and waited beside my desk for Captain Manning, holding towels I'd given them for their bloody faces. I asked them why they fought so much and Alex said he hated niggers and Franklin said he hated spics, and then they stood up and went at it again. I got between them and pushed them apart. Captain Manning opened his door, invited them in, gave them doughnuts from his desk.

That afternoon, Terrell Becker, a second grade teacher, was caught taping his students to their desks so they wouldn't wander around the room while he was talking. Captain Manning told him not to do that anymore, it could be misconstrued. About that time, Harold Owen, one of Becker's students, was standing in the middle of the hall, blowing up a condom like it was a balloon. I said, "Harold, why are you blowing up that condom like it's a balloon?"

Harold said, "What's a condom?"

In the last hour of the day, Christie Skelton came to me, complaining that her head was hot. I made her lie across three chairs, then put a damp cloth on her forehead and fed her aspirin. When Captain Manning came out of his office, he frowned at her and patted her head. Christie looked at him with eyes that called him a phony bastard, and I loved her for it.

I took her home that afternoon because she didn't want to ride the bus and she said her mother would be sleeping. She lived in a trailer park of dirt yards where dogs were chained to concrete steps and shirtless boys walked in packs, carrying pieces of stripped bamboo they'd carved into makeshift spears.

"That's mine," she said. She pointed to a green trailer in a shady back corner. A Pinto was in front of it, burnt deep brown from fire, windows blown, tires flattened. I asked Christie what happened to it.

"My mama's new boyfriend set it on fire so she couldn't go nowhere."

That Friday night, I went to Ray's house for dinner. His place smelled good—like lavender potpourri, and it was clean. He'd lit a couple of candles and had classical music playing. It was the Friday night before the fish-fry, and Ray assured me that everything was fine. He gave me a glass of wine and told me to sit at the table while he finished cooking broiled salmon with asparagus.

Over dinner, Ray told me about his sister who had died ten years before, when she was eighteen and Ray was twenty-four. She had been accepted to a college out west on a full scholarship to study marine biology, and in early August of that year, a day before her goodbye party, a drunk driver hit her head-on at 3:30 in the afternoon when she was coming home from her summer job at the chicken plant. While Ray talked about the toll it had taken on his mother, he started crying. He wiped both cheeks with his napkin, kept talking, and never apologized for crying. After dinner, he put on a vinyl LP of Fats Domino. He sang along and danced in semi-circles around his living room. *You used to cry, every time it rained. You used to cry so much, it was a crying shame.* He had a certain gracefulness about him, and I decided then that because I'd eventually be leaving Dunbar Creek and because it'd been a full year since I'd been touched, and because Ray was a sweet man with a soft voice, that I would let him dance me down the narrow hall and move me to his bed. He unbuttoned my blouse while he kissed my neck.

"Ray," I said.

"Yes, baby," he whispered. He moved his tongue around my ear and softly bit my lobe.

"You're sure everything's ready for the fish-fry?"

"I took care of everything, Josephine."

"Did you get some water pumps and a seine net and a couple of gas-heated deep fryers?"

He pulled off my blouse and dropped it on the floor. "I sure did," he said. He pulled his boots off and dropped them on my blouse. He unbuttoned my pants and pulled down my zipper.

He said, "I got us two five-horse-powered water pumps with fifty feet of four-inch hose." He stood at the end of the bed to pull off my jeans, his large and hairy stomach noticeable for the first time.

"Ray," I said.

"Yes, baby?"

"Could you take off my shoes?"

He took off my shoes and jeans and I unfastened my bra. He ran his fingers down the length of my thigh and back up again and it occurred to me that his hands were smooth, free of the calluses many men contract from the work they do.

He said, "I myself happen to own *two* gas-heated deep fryers, along with two ten-gallon pots and all the seasoning we'll need. I figured we'd need some volunteers, too." He separated my legs with his knee and ran his fingers along the inside of my thigh.

"That's good," I said.

"I figured about twenty men ought to be enough," he whispered. "Some to drain the pond, some to clean the fish, some to cook the fish." He bit my ear again and pressed a finger into me, moving slowly; breathing deeply.

"Will they be there at eight a.m.?"

"Yes ma'am," he said. "About the same time we'll be there, if you'd like to stay here tonight, I mean—we could ride over together."

"Someone's making grits? And coleslaw? Hushpuppies?"

"I took care of everything, Josephine." He hugged me tightly then and brought himself into me. He went slow and looked me in the eyes. Fats Domino sang from the front of the trailer and a gentle breeze blew through an open window.

The next morning, we stopped at his favorite diner for breakfast. I ordered coffee. Ray ordered over-easy eggs and grits and bacon, which he cut up and stirred together, head lowered over his plate, hat lowered over his eyes.

He said, "You know the interesting thing about a roach?"

"I'm afraid I don't, Ray."

"If you was to take and cut his head off, how do you think he'd die? I mean, what would be the official cause of death listed on the coroner's report?"

I pointed to the corner of my mouth so Ray would know on the corner of his mouth was stuck a piece of egg and grit. He wiped it away, and smiled, revealing more eggs and grits.

"I give up," I said.

"Go ahead and guess."

"I don't want to guess."

"Go ahead. Just guess."

"Severed spinal cord?"

"Nope."

"Blood loss?"

"Nope."

"Loss of oxygen to the brain?"

"Nope."

"I give up."

"You want me to tell you?"

"Please."

"Starvation. He'd starve to death. Isn't that something?"

"That's something."

We rode in Ray's truck from the diner to the school. The floorboard was piled high in trash, and the engine rattled loudly, and even though I couldn't make out what he was saying, he kept talking, looking at me from time to time, toothpick in place. I looked out the window at all the small and crooked houses I'd long since memorized. Yards littered with toys, torn trampolines, above-ground pools. Dogs everywhere, who seemed to know my name, lazed on porches and in yards.

The fish-fry was held behind the school, where the children took recess. The pond was in the rear corner of the field, in the crook of the right angle where the thick woods came together. Ray held my hand as we walked between several rows of picnic tables which had been perfectly aligned, topped with red and black checkered tablecloths.

A group of men were gathered at the pond, talking and laughing. When we got close enough, they shouted at Ray. I tried to take my hand away, but he held too tight. Ray joked with them about what the holdup was. They said they were waiting for his slow ass to show up and tell them what to do. Ray told them they wouldn't be able to find their assholes if it weren't for their fingers, and everyone laughed and Ray let go my hand. He looked at his watch and said, "Hell-fire, we may as well get to it."

Someone mentioned all the turtles that had surfaced during the final day of draining. No one had expected there to be so many. They lined every bank of the pond in rows, like spectators filling bleachers. Ray said they'd have to be destroyed because they wouldn't survive now without their water and the fish that kept them alive, and the men moaned because of the extra work this meant.

Ray walked to a seine net and the men followed him. It looked like a long tennis net with posts spread every three feet. Twelve men pulled off their shoes and socks and rolled up their pants legs to the knees. They each grabbed a post on the seine net and entered the water, Ray coaching them from the bank to go slow and easy.

A group of women, wives of these men, most likely, sat in lawn chairs a hundred feet away. They stared at me. Behind them, at the far end of the pond, two big funeral tents had been erected. Beneath the tents were three tables holding deep pots I imagined were full of grits and slaw. About forty gallons of tea covered the last table, and next to them were three fish coolers packed with ice. Two gas fryers were set up between the tables and the pond, metal trays next to them layered in paper towels. A fiberglass cabinet holding two sinks for cleaning fish was set up closer to the pond. The water pumps were turned off, hoses removed and pushed out of the way.

The women stared at me as I walked toward the empty lawn chair in their circle. They looked so comfortable I wondered if they'd ever move again. I sat and smiled at each of them.

"That's Nadine's chair," the lady next to me said. "She's gone to get some Skin So Soft."

The gnats were swarming around our arms and faces and the women held deep frowns while they batted them away. I complimented them on their layout, but they kept frowning from the gnats. We watched the men push the seine net across the pond.

A lady to my right turned to me, her face lit up by the flash of something important. She said, "Is your mama and daddy Audrey and Hubert Haven, worships over at First Church of God in Dunbar?"

"Yes," I said. "That's them."

"Where do you worship?" another lady asked me. "Have you found a home?"

I looked out at the field to see if Nadine was returning. She wasn't.

"Different places," I said. "Here and there. Nowhere in particular."

The women frowned and looked toward the pond.

It took half an hour for the men to push the net into the farthest corner of the pond. They shoved their posts deep into the mud and leaned on them to keep the net sturdy while a separate group of men waded into the water and scooped up the fish with nets and bare hands, tossing them to another group of men who skulled them with ax-handles to keep them from flopping back into the water. There was tremendous whooping and hollering over a few catfish that had grown enormous. They lifted them in the air and called them pet names like Shamu and Jaws.

"They're not good to eat once they get that big," one woman said. "They get too tough."

"You-know-who will eat them," another woman said, and the others nodded.

A group of musicians arrived, carrying equipment to another funeral tent set up in the middle of the field. The women identified them: Larry Evans carried a banjo, Luther Johnson carried a fiddle, Tiny Brown carried an upright bass and a man named Boy Carver carried a microphone and a PA. I assumed Ray had arranged for them to come.

The fish cleaners skinned the cats and scaled the bream, cutting off heads and slicing bellies, dipping what remained into buckets of water to wash them clean. Ray rolled fish in a tub of flour and corn meal, laughing over some joke I wasn't close enough to hear.

The field was full by ten-thirty. Families emptied from the backs of pickup trucks, carrying coolers, lawn chairs, blankets. All the teachers in the school system came with their families, and all the administrators and school board members came with theirs. The mayor and the city and county commissioners came with their families and the sheriff and his deputies came with theirs. Every official in the county was soon there, and so, it seemed, was every citizen who had ever voted for them.

Captain Manning found me and asked if I'd stand at the end of the farthest table to collect $6.95 from every person coming down the line. The women from the lawn chairs served slaw and grits and tea. Larry Evans plucked his banjo and Boy Carver's voice carried high and lonesome across the field, singing "I Hear a Sweet Voice Calling."

Captain Manning gave me a cigar box full of dollar bills and nickels for making change, and then stood beside me, laughing it up with everyone who passed with their styrofoam containers piled high with food. He told Lester Mangram he ought to get hold of a wheelbarrow to save him some trips. Lester said he could probably use one later to haul off his wife with. Then he winked at me. Russell Ferguson paid his money and asked Captain where was the goddamned beer.

Captain said, "Russell, you can't drink beer on school grounds at a family function like this. But if it'll kill you to do without one before noon, then go out to the parking lot and get one from the cooler in the back of my truck and put it in the cup you got your tea in, and take this extra cup and bring me back one too."

Russell laughed and did as he was told.

The sun was cruel, even beneath the tents. Captain Manning kept sending men back to his truck with empty cups and they kept returning with full cups, which he passed among the cleaners and cooks. Boy Carver sang "The Unclouded Day." Then he sang "Life's Railway to Heaven."

I took money from everyone in Dunbar Creek. I took money from all the people who had ever once ignored me while I went through school. They smiled and laughed and gave me money, saying we ought to get together soon, and I agreed without meaning it either. My old teachers patronized me with praise about how far I'd come. Some of them gave me ten dollar bills and said not to worry with the change, and they paused a beat in front of Captain Manning to receive his blessing.

My family gave me money too. Captain Manning told my father how valuable I was to the school system, how they'd be lost without me. My father looked genuinely proud, and this made me sad, because I knew he was defining me then through Captain Manning's eyes. Aunts and uncles carried their plates and gave me money, each of them asking how long I planned to be the old maid of the family. My cousins gave me money, balancing paper plates and babies. They spoke to their children the way you speak to puppies, and I turned quickly to receive the next person in line.

Captain Manning replaced the cigar box with a five-gallon bucket, and when I made change, fish guts stuck to dollar bills. Boy Carver sang "Swing Low Sweet Chariot," then he sang "I Saw the Light," and the cloggers stepped forward to kick up dust. Captain Manning sank his fat hand down into the five-gallon bucket full of money and laughed. Then his face dropped and he looked horrified.

"What's wrong?" I said.

"We forgot to say the goddamned blessing."

He looked out at all the families in the field, people propped on elbows, lying on their backs and sides, gorged and lazy. He went in search of Reverend Baker. The women at the tables who had been dipping grits and slaw started straightening up while they fed themselves. It occurred to me that I had not eaten and was not hungry.

Across the back side of the pond, a group of school boys were destroying turtles with ax handles and baseball bats. Those without tools lofted turtles toward those with tools, sending shards of shells flying into the woods. Once I saw them, I could identify the sound I'd been hearing, even as the music played, but which I could not locate until that moment.

Captain Manning waited for Boy Carver to finish "I'll Fly Away," then he borrowed Boy's microphone and announced that he'd intended to save the blessing for last to make sure everyone was made happy with food. He handed the microphone to Reverend Baker, who cleared his voice, then blessed Boy Carver and his band, praising the Holy Ghost's gift of music.

Ray stumbled up to me then, eyes red from drinking. He held a piece of fish before my mouth. I shook my head, but he raised it to my mouth anyway, insisting. I chewed and swallowed. He raised his cup of beer to my mouth and I sipped from it.

Rev. Baker thanked God for giving us good weather. He asked God to look favorably on all the people of Dunbar Creek who had come to give fellowship on behalf of the children. Ray removed his hat and placed it over his heart. He closed his eyes and stumbled. His breathing deepened, as if on the verge of sleep.

I looked across the field for Christie Skelton, and found her finally, sitting on the far side of the pond in front of the boys who were killing turtles. She was facing me, though her eyes seemed locked on the empty pond between us.

Rev. Baker asked God to bless those who had organized the day's events, particularly Captain Manning and John Hampton. Ray rocked back on his heels. The ladies leaned their tired bodies on the tables for support, heads bowed.

Rev. Baker asked God to look favorably upon all the employees of the school system whose contributions rarely got recognized: the bus drivers, the cafeteria workers, the custodians, the substitute teachers, the recess monitors and the handymen.

I looked out at the field full of people and imagined them all gathered here for some similar function five years away. They might try to remember what had brought them last together and then they'd pause, mouth full of food. Someone might eventually recall a fragment of the truth, saying something about the girl who drowned at school that time and then they'd nod and look sad and resume their chewing.

The boys who'd been killing turtles were now stalking them in the shallow woods. Lou Duncan buried the butt end of a pitchfork in the ground, and stuck a turtle on the prongs. Its arms and legs were moving as if it meant to swim.

Burgundy puddles of light pressed against a distant row of pines. I saw a version of myself walk through the crowd, across the parking lot to the road and down that road to another road that would lead, eventually, to an interstate that would take me to another life. But it was just a version of myself, and when Reverend Baker finally said "amen" and all the heads rose and the eyes opened, I saw myself standing next to Ray while Boy Carver started singing "The Great Speckled Bird."

Ray said, "Josephine?" He put his cap back on, tightened it down, then took it off again. He held it in front of his crotch with both hands and gave me a look that scared me. He said, "Would you marry me?" He put a hand on my shoulder and squeezed it. He said, "We're not getting any younger, Josephine—I want to start a family, and I know you'd be a wonderful mother."

I looked toward the field of people. His question knocked the wind out of me. I wanted to object strongly and let him down easily, which meant I didn't know what to say. His hand was heavy. I looked at him and opened my mouth to tell him no, but nothing came. I felt weighed down by a thousand years' worth of heat and history, and all my words for "no" had vanished.

Behind Ray, some fifteen feet away, Captain Manning stuck the tail-end of a fish into his mouth and smiled at me. I looked at Ray and opened my mouth again.

"Don't answer right now," Ray said. "I just know that I could love you a long time right here in Dunbar Creek without ever needing anything. It's just that when I know something, I know it, you know?"

I nodded, objecting. I opened my mouth and closed it.

"We'll talk later," Ray said. "I was thinking on the way home, we might ride by and visit my ailing mother. I know she'd be proud to meet you."

I said no, but it came out as a whisper, and he'd already turned and started talking to Captain Manning about how well everything had gone and what a beautiful day it was. I looked toward Christie, who was still sitting on the far side of the pond, close to the woods, staring toward me. She was a hundred yards or more away, and people were between us, but I waved. First, I waved with my hand beside my shoulder, then I raised my arm above my head and waved, then I stood on my tiptoes and waved until she lifted her right hand, just barely to the shoulder, and wiggled her fingers back at me.

Last Words
of the Holy Ghost

Harold's mother, Jude, said he shouldn't worry about getting saved or baptized or having to speak in tongues if all he cared about was sex. She sat on the couch in her robe, applying red polish to her nails after a day of oil painting. Her third husband, Clay Carter, occupied his recliner, cleaning his teeth and gums with his battery-powered brush. Harold lay between them on the floor, staring at the divot he'd made in the ceiling with his three-iron. His pit bull puppy, Maggie, snored against his side while Dan Rather, the evening news anchor, talked of chaos in Guatemala.

Most of all, his mother said, Harold shouldn't want sex with the likes of Rose Carver, 15, whose mother insisted that Harold, 14, should accept Jesus Christ as his personal savior before he and Rose could go to a goddamn movie together.

Clay said, "I don't think it would hurt him." He talked without removing his brush.

"You don't think *what* would hurt him?" Jude said. "Getting saved or having sex?"

"Being baptized doesn't always lead to sex," Clay mumbled.

"What else do you think he wants?"

Clay didn't answer.

Jude said, "Really, Harold. You can do better than Rose Carver."

Clay removed his toothbrush. "I like Rose," he said. "She's grown up tough, which means she won't fall apart on you when the smallest little thing goes to hell."

Harold's mother gave Clay the look, heat simmering behind her eyes.

Clay reinserted his brush and looked back toward Dan Rather, who said things were going to hell in Guatemala.

Harold would see Rose Sunday, two days after he and Clay rode ninety miles inland—from their coastal Georgia home—to Clay's farm, where Rose lived in a trailer with her parents. The Carvers took care of the hundred acres, the thirty cows, and Harold's horse, Henry, that Clay had given him three years ago, before marrying Jude. During the past year, Harold had come to love Rose Carver. Between monthly visits, he and Rose exchanged love letters.

"I do *not* fall apart," his mother said, "when the smallest little thing goes to hell."

Clay removed his brush. "No one said you fall apart."

"You implied it."

Clay reinserted his brush and lifted his eyebrows, implying that he did not deny having implied such. Dan Rather said the killing would likely continue through the weekend and for years to come.

Jude said, "Harold, you shouldn't waste yourself on trashy girls."

"He's learning things," Clay said.

"Not from the right people."

In Harold's last letter to Rose, he'd agreed to being saved, and to getting baptized, and to speaking in tongues if that's what it took for him and Rose to be alone. He imagined a movie leading to a kiss and the kiss leading, eventually, to sex. He had never kissed or been kissed, but he'd been ready for sex for several years.

"And you've already been baptized," his mother said.

"He doesn't remember that." Clay didn't remove his brush, and then he did. He said, "You're supposed to be baptized at an age when you can remember."

"You should be baptized as early as possible," Jude said. "To remove original sin."

Clay said, "No kid comes into the world with sin on his head."

"Mine did."

"Maybe yours did, but—"

Clay inserted his toothbrush and turned toward the news again.

"But *what?*" Jude said.

"Nothing," Clay said. "Harold's head is okay."

In Rose's last letter, she mentioned a new bikini she wanted to wear when she visited Harold at the beach, but she'd like to show it to him earlier if he didn't mind, so long as he went to church first.

"And Harold?" his mother said. "Catholics do not speak in tongues. That's something we just don't do."

"The Pope does," Clay said. "The Pope knows several languages."

"Don't be disrespectful."

Harold had decided that as soon as he got saved and baptized and spoke in tongues, he would buy a calendar so he and Rose could document the number of times per day they had sex and then show it to jealous friends, saying five on this day, six on that day, then he'd yawn because sex would be so common.

"Maybe you could go with us," Clay said to Jude.

"No. I'm through with that place."

Harold knew his mother had grown bored with the farm and that she liked occasional weekends to herself so she could paint her seascapes and take them to the island gallery where tourists bought them as fast as she could get them there—a gallery owned by a well-dressed man who kissed her hand.

Harold also knew that she didn't like Larry Carver, Rose's father, who kept pit bulls locked in cages behind his trailer. Once, they'd seen Larry driving down the dirt road with six dogs tied to his truck's rear bumper. "Jogging the dogs," he called it. And she didn't like that Larry had recently given Harold a pit bull puppy with cropped ears and tail, though she admitted the dog would have a better life with Harold.

There were lots of things his mother told Harold she didn't like: the occasional screaming that came from Larry and Susie's trailer, a hundred yards from the farmhouse, Susie coming in the morning to apologize for the previous night's noise, sometimes confessing details in front of Harold—that she'd met Larry, for instance, when she was fifteen and he was twenty-five, and he'd just wandered into town from Wisconsin on his motorcycle, running from some trouble he never explained. Her family told her not to marry him, she said, so she did.

And his mother didn't like Rose, with her skimpy clothes, who seemed unconcerned with doing any better for herself than her parents had done for themselves. But what his mother said she liked least was the way she saw Harold changing. He kept a toothpick in his mouth and wore caps, flannel shirts, and a pair of work boots Clay bought him. He said *dinner* for lunch and *supper* for dinner, and he packed his sentences with double negatives and *ain'ts*. On her last visit to the farm, Harold had asked her not to sound so fancy with the way she talked around the Carvers.

Now, she sighed while screwing the cap onto her fingernail polish. "If that girl talks you into anything, Harold—for God's sake, use a condom."

"I'll agree with that," Clay said.

Harold rubbed Maggie's cropped ears and stared at the hole he'd made in the ceiling when his three-iron flew out of his hands. His mother had bought the clubs so Clay could teach him how to golf. They played one round and went once to the driving range, but Harold's grip still needed work. He was fully prepared to give up golf in favor of farming anyway. He wanted to be the kind of man Rose Carver would respect.

That Sunday morning, Harold sat in a pew between Rose and Susie Carver. Rose's hair smelled like strawberries. He stole glimpses of flesh between her knees and feet and imagined caressing her long legs. Then he imagined her legs from the knee up, and by then it was too late to stop his erection, so he put a Bible in his lap, and Rose yawned for the third time, which made him wonder whether she even liked him.

Susie patted him on the knee. She said, "Harold? After today, you'll feel a love that cannot be stolen."

"I'm ready," Harold said.

Then Uncle Elmer stood from the front pew and faced his congregation. He was Susie's older brother, tall and thin, wet hair combed back and white collar open at the neck. He stood on tiptoes and raised his palms for people to stand, then everyone started singing loudly, especially the red-robed choir, while a tall-haired lady pounded an upright piano. Susie sang loudly and Rose sang softly. Their voices were beautiful, and the voices of the choir were beautiful, the piano was beautiful, and the slanted light coming through the oval windows was beautiful. Rose shared her hymnal, brushing against Harold's shoulder, but Harold didn't sing. He knew he'd sound bad, so he moved his lips and listened to everyone else sing about a closer walk with thee, a phrase that sometimes got repeated, which sounded beautiful.

After the song, after everyone was seated, Elmer talked excitedly in a strange accent. Rose said he'd traveled to England several years ago to look for his ancestors and came home sounding funny. He paced, sweating as he talked about the horrible heat of hell. He talked about the world's worst sinners, the media, who pushed ideas of sex into the minds of children, which reminded Harold to look at Rose's legs again. She slid her fingers beneath Harold's thigh, and the blood came surging too fast for him to stop the swelling and Susie said, "Glory."

It looked like Elmer might have a heart attack. And then suddenly he was crying. He closed his eyes and dabbed his head with his handkerchief. When he opened his eyes, he stared straight at Harold, as if he were the only one in church. Rose moved her hand.

Elmer whispered into his microphone. He said, "God has just told me a secret."

"Yes, he did," someone said.

Elmer stared at Harold so long that Harold's heart started pounding.

Elmer said, "God told me that there is a lost young soul in His house today who has come here for deliverance."

Harold's heart pounded so hard he decided God's hand was squeezing it. The choir started singing softly with the piano that was playing softly, and Elmer's voice got louder. Harold decided his heart was being squeezed because of the sinful things he'd been thinking.

Elmer said, "God has just informed me that He is asking this young person to come forward today so He can remove his heart of stone and replace it with a heart of flesh. God said He will give this young man a new heart and a new spirit with it."

Susie moved her legs. Harold's heart pounded harder.

"Come," Elmer said. "And give your heart to Jesus."

Harold went. The choir and the piano grew louder while Harold walked toward Elmer. Someone said, "Glory Hallelujah." Elmer met Harold, grabbed his arm, and guided him to the far side of the altar, where he pulled back a red curtain to reveal a glass tank of waist-high water, large enough to hold a shark. Elmer told Harold to remove his socks and shoes and to climb into the tank, and then he said he'd be right back. Harold looked over his shoulder toward Rose, who might've been smiling, though it was hard to tell, and then at Susie, who had one hand raised toward the ceiling. The choir sang and the piano played. Harold thought of Rose while he removed his socks and shoes. He thought of her while he rolled up the navy slacks he wore for his Catholic school uniform, and he thought of her as he climbed the three steps and descended into the cold water. He imagined holding onto Rose in the ocean while she wrapped her legs around him, water up to their necks to hide the sex they'd be having. Then another erection started up, so Harold looked for Elmer, who reappeared in a pair of green waders.

Elmer climbed into the tank. He put his hands on top of Harold's head and started praying fast and loud. He moved one hand to the back of Harold's neck and put his other hand on Harold's chest and pushed him backwards into the water too fast for Harold to pinch his nose, and he came up quickly, snorting and coughing, but it didn't stop Elmer's string of words, nor did it break Elmer's grip on Harold's neck, a grip so tight that Harold imagined Blackjack Mulligan applying The Claw, a wrestling hold that made its victims lose consciousness every Saturday afternoon on Channel 2.

Elmer pronounced Harold saved in the name of Jesus and proclaimed that his body was now a vessel for the Holy Ghost. Elmer hugged Harold. After a few seconds, Elmer released him long enough for Harold to wipe his face and push his hair back. He smiled toward Rose, then climbed out of the tank and down the steps, where several women covered him in towels while speaking in a foreign language.

Elmer said, "Open your mouth, son. Open your mouth and let loose the Holy Ghost."

Harold opened his mouth. Nothing happened. He put a finger in his ear to dislodge some water, and he closed his eyes to concentrate, but no words came. Then a picture appeared to him—Rose's legs—and he imagined that very soon she would let him touch her body for several hours straight, and he imagined how her face might look when it was lit with pleasure, and he imagined what she would do to his body for years to come, so he opened his mouth and made his lips into the shape they'd formed the previous summer when he'd learned from his father in North Carolina how to talk like an auctioneer, and the sound that came was a language like the women were using. The first sounds inspired him, so he kept his eyes closed and very soon he was stringing together words that came spewing from what he assumed to be *his* tongue, words rolling in a frenzied rush with no effort at all, except to remember some of the filler words used in auctioneering, such as "bidbuysell."

He wanted it to stop, the storm of words, but it wouldn't stop because his body had taken over. Then he opened his eyes and saw a woman staring at him while she too spoke the words, and then he stopped.

"I think he had it," one woman said. "I heard it there for a second."

"I heard it, too," another woman said.

The music played while people hugged him and congratulated him all the way out of the church and into the bright parking lot. Rose came through the crowd to give the longest hug, and she tightened the towel around his shoulders. "*Now* we can go to the show," she said. "And do all sorts of things."

Bright sunlight streamed from the sky, and Harold's heart burned with promise.

On the way home, Harold and Clay talked easily for ninety miles, occasionally singing along to country music tear-jerkers and pointing to odd sites, like a mule tied to a front porch or a shirtless old man smoking a cigarette beneath a puny shade tree. Monday, they'd resume their routines—Clay would go to work as a computer programmer at the seafood plant, and Harold would go to his 8th grade class at St. Francis Xavier, talking nonchalantly about his new girlfriend. But on this Sunday afternoon, Highway 32 carved a map in Harold's mind that made him sink into the land. And Clay talked to Harold like an adult friend, sharing ideas without making it sound like advice, and Harold loved him for it.

Clay said, "I wonder if she's the type that you might keep one eye on while the other eye plays the field."

"That's what I always do," Harold said. "I always play the field." But he was lying. He wanted Rose immediately, exclusively, and for a long time. As soon as he got home, he planned to write her a letter saying so.

Clay said, "You might be careful how you tell your mother about it. You don't want her thinking that being Catholic isn't good enough for you. At the very least, you might tell her I had nothing to do with your clothes getting wet."

Clay and his mother fought too frequently. One recent morning Harold heard them in the kitchen while he walked down the hall, his mother asking Clay how she was supposed to feel, exactly, when he said, "Eck," after she licked his ear. Harold rounded the corner then and walked between them, went outside and climbed aboard the school bus his mother drove every morning and every afternoon.

When they got home, Harold went to the side porch, where she was painting white specks on the tops of waves breaking behind a lighthouse.

Harold said, "I got saved and baptized and spoke in tongues."

His mother poked her bottom lip out and frowned. She said, "Oh, Harold-honey. What will become of you at high noon when you carry your ladder to women's windows?"

"What?"

"Don't tell your grandmother." Then she went back to her painting.

Harold's grandmother, also his godmother and next-door neighbor, said ten rosaries a day. She gave Harold Holy Cards and offered each week to take him to confession. He hoped very soon he'd have something to confess.

Three weeks later, Rose and her father picked Harold up at Clay's farmhouse. The bed of Larry's truck held pens crammed with dogs. Rose sat in the middle. They were quiet until they got to Jeff Davis Memorial Highway, and then Rose apologized for the heater not working.

"I'm not cold," Harold said.

"Yes you are," Rose answered.

Larry said, "Son? How's that little bitch behaving for you?"

It took Harold a second to realize that Larry was talking about his dog.

"Just fine," Harold said. "I got that bitch behaving real good." He nodded toward Larry and looked back at the road.

Larry said, "What you name her?"

Harold wanted to lie, but he couldn't think of anything, so he told the truth. "Maggie."

Larry laughed so loud it hurt Harold's ears. He said, "*Maggie?*"

"My mom's idea," Harold said, which was true—after a nun she'd known at boarding school, but he instantly felt ashamed for blaming her.

"Maggie's a cute name," Rose said. "Better than *bitch.*"

Harold peeked at Larry's left hand sitting atop the steering wheel—his thumb was missing. He'd noticed this before, and asked Clay about it, but Clay didn't know what had happened. It was the kind of information someone ought to volunteer, he said, and Larry never volunteered anything. Harold imagined a dog had bitten it off.

Rose didn't want popcorn or drinks. She led Harold into the movie and close to the front and to the far left, all the way against the wall, which was a bad angle to the screen, but a good place to kiss in the dark. He thought, too late, that he should be sitting on the outside, but he didn't say anything. Rose sat very still. She looked over her shoulder once, then back to the white screen. Harold wiped his hand on his jeans and moved his arm to the armrest, so it would be closer to Rose's hand. He would reach for it as soon as it got dark. He figured on five minutes of hand-holding before he put his arm around her. In his mind, he rehearsed lifting his arm over her head. Twenty minutes into the movie, he'd kiss her. When he pictured this, his heart started beating as hard as it had in church. He licked his dry lips and swallowed.

When the lights went down, Rose said, "I have to go to the bathroom."

She stood into a crouch and ducked down the aisle. Harold waited for her to come back.

He waited longer than he thought was normal. He started looking over his shoulder so he could wave as she wandered down the dark aisle. But he never saw her. His stomach started hurting. He looked over his shoulder a few more times. He waited. Then he decided he'd go to the lobby to find her, but the lobby was empty. He looked through the glass wall into the parking lot, but no one was out there. He shuffled back to his seat, looking down all the dark aisles to other seats she might've moved to. He saw two couples kissing, but he couldn't see their faces.

He slumped in his seat and held his stomach. On the screen, he saw a movie projected from his mind about about a boy who sits alone in a theatre, abandoned by a beautiful girl. Sound came from the actors' mouths, but he couldn't make out their words.

When the movie ended, he followed hand-holding couples toward the lobby. Everyone could see he was alone. Rose sat on a bench beside the exit. Harold stood in front of the glass, looking into the parking lot for her father, giving Rose a chance to say something. She looked at her fingernails, she looked at the big clock over the concession stand, and she looked back into the parking lot. Harold stood silently for five more minutes, arms crossed. It was Susie, in her four-door Dodge, who finally pulled up.

Harold got in back, saying nothing.

Susie said, "How was the movie?"

"Sad," Rose said. "It was a sad movie." She sounded very sincere.

Susie looked in the mirror to see if Harold agreed, but Harold ignored her. He looked out his window.

"It must've been sad," Susie said. "Harold looks like he's about to cry."

"It was sad," Rose said again.

Susie said, "Sometimes this life ain't funny, is it Harold?"

"No ma'am, it's not," he said.

No one said anything else until Rose and Susie said goodnight at the same time.

Susie said, "Harold, you want us to pick you up in the morning for church?"

"No," he said. "No, thank you." He closed the car door and walked up the steps.

Sunday, Harold told Clay what had happened. Clay said he was sorry, and then he said he didn't know what to say. They rode silently through a series of one-light towns separated by woods and fields. Harold kept one hand on Maggie, asleep against his leg. Clay stopped at a convenience store. He said, "What we need is a couple Yoo-hoos."

He gave Harold one, and they started down the road again, back through the thinning pine woods dotted every now and then with a parked yellow machine that held a tree pincher like a crab claw. Harold's heart was a stump. His heart was the hole where the stump used to be. He had an overwhelming desire to get run over by a train. He wanted to stand in the middle of the tracks at midnight while he stared into the oncoming light and stick his chest out to receive it.

Clay said, "What we need is some Hank Williams."

Harold wanted to say No, please, no, but he didn't say anything, so Clay pushed in the 8-track. Hank sang "Alone and Forsaken." He sang "Can't Get You off My Mind." He sang "Your Cheatin' Heart" and "Cold, Cold Heart."

Clay said, "Isn't that better?"

Harold said it was. His Yoo-hoo was empty. They were almost home.

Clay said, "Son? In twenty years you won't even remember her name."

Harold wondered if his heart would hold out for twenty years.

Clay said, "I won't lie to you: There are times in this life when you'll get shit on. All you can do is wash it off and move away from the shitter and refuse to be shit on again. And I'll tell you what my daddy told me: It's better to be pissed off than to be pissed on."

There was much talk of shit and piss, and Harold started feeling better.

"Don't tell your mom I used that language."

Harold didn't tell his mother anything. He found her on the side porch, standing in front of her easel while she laughed into the phone. When Harold stepped onto the porch, she said "Bons-wa" into the phone and hung it up. Then she said "Bon-sure" to Harold.

She said, "You look a little sad, sugarbear. What happened?"

Harold looked at the painting. He looked at the nets on a distant shrimp boat that sat inside a strip of light on the horizon's edge, a long way from the lighthouse.

"Nothing," he said.

"The heart is a lonely hunter, isn't it?"

"I don't know."

"Is there something you want to tell me?" she said.

Harold didn't want to volunteer anything about his shit-stained heart.

"French is a beautiful language," his mother said. "Isn't it?"

Harold walked away.

Three days later, he got a letter from Rose full of explanations and apologies. A friend of hers was in the hospital, she said, so she'd arranged for another friend to pick her up at the movie so they could visit the first friend because Rose's mother hated both friends since they weren't saved. Rose said she hadn't been able to eat or sleep and she hated herself for the cruel thing she'd done, and she begged for another chance so she could prove she was not a bad person. She said she cared very deeply for Harold. She talked of coming to the beach over the summer and mentioned her bikini. She wanted to get into the water with him, she said, out to where no one could see what they might be doing. "Please," she said. "Do the Christian thing and forgive me?"

When he finished reading the letter, he carried Maggie to the side porch where his mother was painting another seagull over another ocean while Neil Diamond sang "Song Sung Blue."

Jude said, "Oh Harold, my lovely string bean, my blueberry prince. Why so sad?"

He carried Maggie back to his bedroom and labored over a letter saying he would allow Rose Carver one more chance.

A month later, Rose's father dropped them off. They went to the same seats, this time with popcorn. Rose reached for Harold's sweaty hand. She held his hand and caressed his forearm with her other hand. Adult actors kissed on the big screen and laughed between kisses to bouncy music. Rose leaned over and kissed Harold on the lips. All the blood in his body stormed his crotch, and his heart pounded like it had in church.

Rose said, "Harold? I have to go to the bathroom." She kissed him again. "I promise," she said. "I'll be right back."

"I believe you," Harold said.

But she never came back. He did not look for her. He dropped the full tub of popcorn on the floor and slumped in his seat. On the big screen he saw a picture of himself sitting next to an empty seat. Sound came from the actors' mouths, but all he heard was a woman laughing and a man calling himself a fool.

When the movie ended, Harold followed the hand-holding couples to the lobby and looked for Rose. She wasn't there. He looked through the glass into the parking lot, and after a few minutes a truck with tall tires and a loud muffler pulled up and let Rose out. The driver looked like a high school senior or someone just out of high school. He had stubble on his face and a football player's neck. The guy looked at Harold through the glass, gave him a wink and half a smile, and then sped off, muffler rumbling.

Rose came inside and sat on the bench. She looked at the clock above the concession stand, out at the parking lot, at her fingernails, and back to the parking lot. Harold crossed his arms and waited for her to acknowledge him, but she never did.

Her father picked them up. The pens in his truck bed were full of panting dogs. Rose rode in the middle, popping her chewing gum.

Her father said, "I didn't do worth a shit tonight; how'd y'all do?"

"We did okay," Rose said.

They rode silently down Jeff Davis Memorial Highway, turned onto the dirt road that led to Clay's farm, saying nothing. When Larry stopped, he said, "Rose—walk ol' Harold up to the door there and give him a goodnight kiss."

"I already gave him one, Daddy."

Larry said, "Looks like that's all you get, son." Then he laughed and said so long, and sped off as soon as Harold closed the truck door.

Harold told Clay it had happened again, and again Clay said he didn't know what to say. They rode in silence through one-light towns separated by woods and fields. Harold kept one hand on Maggie, who slept against his leg. Clay stopped at a convenience store. He said, "Let's get a couple Yoo-hoos." Harold never opened his. His heart was a prune. A prune pecked by a bald turkey vulture. His head weighed a hundred pounds. He'd been saved for nothing. A cloud moved through his window and through his eyes and swelled inside his skull. He had an overwhelming desire to find the Tallahatchie bridge that Billy Jo McAllister had jumped from.

Clay said, "Let's see if Hank will help."

Hank sang "You Win Again." Then, halfway into "I'm So Lonesome I Could Cry," Harold let loose a tear from each eye that he didn't bother wiping.

Clay said, "Don't cry yet, Harold. I'm telling you the God's truth—in twenty years you won't know her name. Other problems will come along that will make you forget her. In twenty years, you'll have so many problems you'll wish for younger days. Don't cry yet."

Harold looked at the barren fields and thinning pines and yellow machines.

When Harold walked through the door, he found his mother lying on the couch, laughing into the phone, cigarette in one hand. Into the phone she said "Orv-wa." When she saw Harold, she said, "What happened to you?"

Harold felt like crying again, and it must have shown, because his mother said, "Oh Harold-honey. Don't cry yet, sugarbear."

"Okay," he said. But that's all he said. He didn't want to tell his mother what Rose had done, and he trusted Clay not to tell either. He carried Maggie to his room and did not cry. From down the hall, he heard his mother and Clay begin an argument. The next day, during his first period religion class with Sister Ruth, he wrote Rose a letter, trying to be pissed off. He told her she could find someone else to shit on. He drew a picture of a hand with the middle finger sticking up. He told her that sin looked prettier than she did and that her teeth would soon rot out. He told her she'd always live in that falling-down trailer with her parents, and she'd have ten kids by the time she was twenty. He wrote in his unreadable handwriting for eight pages, and then threw the pages away.

When the school year ended, Harold's father picked him up and took him back to North Carolina for a month-long visit. They stayed in a small apartment with his father's fourth wife, Jane, a serious woman who didn't like Harold being there. One weekend, the three of them went to Tweetsie Railroad in Boone. His father and Jane started an argument before they left that continued once they got there. The argument picked up steam once they boarded the train, and got louder when the fake Indians jumped aboard to rob everyone, and got louder still while the fake sheriff and his fake deputies shot the fake Indians. Then they argued on the way home, where they started drinking, and they kept arguing after Harold went to bed. They seemed to argue over things they'd already argued about, one of those things being his father's secret vasectomy. At three a.m., his father pulled Harold from bed and took him to a one-floor, U-shaped motel, where they stayed two weeks, until it was time for Harold to go home. Every night, Harold drank one beer, because that way, his father said, it wouldn't be habit-forming.

His mother drove from Georgia to retrieve him. On the way home, she told Harold that Clay had moved out.

Harold looked into the woods.

She said she knew Harold and Clay liked each other, and it was all terribly sad, and she was very sorry, she said, but these things happened and they'd survive. The money would be tight, and she'd have to find a full-time job, but they'd survive.

Harold kept his head turned. He wanted to talk to Clay to see if it was true.

His mother said, "I have to tell you something else."

Harold closed his eyes as his mother told him that Maggie had turned up dead one day without a scratch. He stared into the woods, thinking his grandfather might have done it. Maggie had once killed one of his chickens, which made his grandfather angry, so Harold suspected his grandfather had poisoned her.

"I'm sorry, sugarbear," his mother said. "It comes in streaks, doesn't it?"

Harold looked into the moving woods. His heart was a piece of coal. A piece of coal wrapped in a wrinkled map. A twisted and balled-up map lodged between lungs where a piece of coal was burning. A bloodstained map that tore every time he breathed. He wanted to set his heart on fire.

Just below Savannah, fifty miles from home, the full moon perched above the woods to his left, and the sun sank on an even plane toward the woods on his right. The sky was orange and amber; the long June day was ending slowly. His mother leaned over the steering wheel to look. She said, "Isn't that a lovely and heartbreaking sight?"

Harold cried then and couldn't stop crying. He cried so loud and so long that he grew embarrassed in front of his mother. He cried with his eyes closed tight and from his mouth came sobbing noises. He cried himself into little whimpers and got the hiccups. Twenty miles from home, he pulled a napkin from the glovebox, blew his nose, and struggled a long while before his lungs would accept a deep breath.

"I know it's sad, Harold," his mother said. "And I'm very sorry. But before long, maybe we can have some fun together. I have this friend who has a nice boat, and he's offered to take us deep-sea fishing. Wouldn't that be fun?"

Harold looked into the moonlit woods.

"Wouldn't deep-sea fishing be fun, though?"

Harold didn't answer.

His heart was a trout lying in the woods. A sun-baked trout whose mouth kept moving, spilling final words from the Holy Ghost. A trout whose eyes had turned to scales, who couldn't cry enough tears to save itself. He wanted to wander through the woods until he found it. He would put it in his pocket, or wear it around his neck, and present it to the first girl who smiled at him.

Awful Pretty

Just after midnight, for the third straight night, Ma calls and wakes me from my shallow sleep to say she's hearing a strange voice coming from the woods behind her house again, louder this time, and she is scared. I've been telling her it's just an animal, maybe a heartbroken skunk who has lost its mate, but she is past the point of listening.

"Come listen, Benny," she says. "Someone is *singing* out there. I'm not crazy. I can hear perfectly well."

"It's just an animal, Ma." I keep my eyes closed. I yawn. I've been sleep-deprived for a long time myself, for my own good reasons.

"I can't hear you, honey. Take off your mask."

I remove the sleeping mask connected to the oxygen tank Dr. Peikart prescribed for the apnea Dr. Lupi diagnosed three months ago after Dr. Adamczyk watched a video of me sleeping, which showed I had stopped breathing seventeen times within six hours.

"If we don't get some sleep soon," Ma says, "we'll die from insomnia."

The *we* includes Oscar, her goldfish, who is sensitive to stress. When Ma can't sleep, Oscar gets nervous and swims in manic circles.

"Then the blood will be on your hands, Benny. How would you like to live with yourself after that, honey?"

My alarm is set for six a.m. because I have to work for the eleventh straight day. And I'm already feeling the early stages of what is likely a lung infection caught from one of the hundred-plus sickees I admitted to the emergency room during today's twelve-hour shift. If I remain sleep-deprived, my immunities will collapse and this sickness will blossom into a full-blown condition that will render me lifeless for seven to ten days, during which time I'll be tempted to swallow the bottle of temazepam I keep on my bedside table for such occasions, which I came close to doing three months ago, when I was in bed for *thirteen* straight days.

"Come listen, Benny. Your sister's not answering her phone. I called her first, of course. God knows where she's running the streets. Bring your gun."

"I don't have a gun, Ma."

"What kind of man don't have a gun these days? I'm asking for your help, Benny. I haven't been myself since that thing next door. You know that."

I yawn. *That thing next door* happened two months ago when this pretty normal-seeming guy, Wayne Houston, decapitated his seven-year-old disabled son. It made national news. He put his son's decapitated head in his wheelchair and parked the wheelchair at the end of the driveway so the boy's mother could see it when she came home. The *Daily Sun* said that Wayne said, "I wanted his mother to see what she had done. I wanted her to feel stupid."

"I think it's a gospel song," Ma says. "It's awful spooky."

I take my broom handle and my flashlight. I broke my broom last week while I was murdering a spider in the bathroom. The flashlight I keep on my bedside table for late-night bathroom trips. I haven't replaced my nightlight and the spiders keep multiplying, probably from the neighbors' dirty apartments. My best friend, Bruce, who works with me in triage, is married to a woman who lost her foot from a brown recluse bite. They met in a bar, actually, where she used her missing foot as a conversation piece. Bruce promised to cure her phantom pain, and I guess he did, because I attended their wedding fifteen years ago. It was the last joyful thing I witnessed. After that, my father, Dr. Benjamin Bent, Sr., a surgeon, killed himself over a botched operation. A week later, my wife moved to Tokyo with Dr. Maleszewski, taking my daughter, Kimberly, then three years old. My wife claimed I would forever be a hopeless mama's boy. She claimed I was too self-centered to help my own troubled sister, who constantly left whiny messages. She claimed I was in love with Bruce. I denied nothing. I didn't fight for custody. I looked forward to being alone, but when I was alone, I stopped sleeping. I blame the loud neighbors and their loud arguments, which get louder after I bang the walls. And lately, I've had dizzy spells, which Dr. Demaerschalk said she'd like to keep an eye on. Then Dr. Demaerschalk had a stroke. She left her patients unattended and offered no referrals, which I found both inconvenient and unprofessional.

When my wife left, I moved into an apartment complex a half-mile from Ma's house. In the past year, some new neighbors (I suspect the shirtless, tattooed Hispanic kids who like to flaunt their underwear) have committed inexplicable acts of cruelty towards me, such as plastering hateful bumper stickers to my car. Last month, it was this one: "Silly faggot, dicks are for chicks." I covered it with a "People Suck" sticker.

And now, just after midnight, as I stumble toward my car, I find a dead cat on the driver's side windshield—the wild black cat I'd been leaving milk for. A line of blood, still wet, had spilled from one nostril. I stare at its whiskers and its open eyes, its soft paws and its bloody nose, and I bend to vomit. This is what it's come to. I go back to my apartment for a bag, put the kitty in it, tie the bag, then drop it in the dumpster so her body won't be mutilated by wild animals. On the way to Ma's, I plot ways to mutilate the kids who did this.

Behind Ma's house, I crunch dead leaves and stand between her open bedroom window and the woods, wishing I'd worn a coat over the robe I wore over my pajamas. I shine my light into the woods and listen. I don't hear anything.

"Do you hear anything?" Ma yells through her window.

A man says, "Now you've scared it off."

I shine my light at her window. "Is someone in there with you?"

The man says, "Is that him? He took long enough."

"Who's in there?"

"Did you hear the singing?" Ma says. "It sounded like a tormented angel."

I walk to her window. She is seventy, still in better shape than most everyone I know, from the neck down, at least. She gets a little scared at night while she watches her crime shows, but I don't blame her, especially after what happened next door.

When I press my nose to the screen, Ben Gay smacks me at once, along with menthol, moth balls, and some old familiar gloom that knocks me back forty years.

She says, "I can hear you breathing, honey. Is your asthma acting up?"

"He's too fat," the man says. "He was born too fat."

I raise the flashlight, cup my other hand around my left eye and see—sitting on the far edge of the bed with his back facing me, wearing the tank-top T-shirt preferred by older men—an older man.

Ma says, "Turn off that light. You're scaring Oscar."

The man turns his profile toward me.

"Who's that man sitting on your bed?" I say.

"You know Dr. Wright. He delivered you into this world forty-five years ago."

"Hiya, Benjamin. How's things on the first floor?"

"What're you doing in there?"

"I was inspecting your mother's rash, likely caused by an ingrown pubic hair that got infected. I applied some ointment, but we'll have to keep monitoring the situation."

"Did you hear it, Benny? That singing? Do you think I'm crazy, now, Mr. Big-shot Triage Man? Wasn't it awful pretty?"

I hold on to the side of the house. I say, "We'll have to keep monitoring the situation."

"Listen to you," she says. "You sound just like a doctor."

"I have to go now."

"Good night, honey," Ma says.

"Good night, *honey*," Dr. Wright says.

I try to sleep—even a nightmare would be nice, to get my mind off Dr. Wright's house call—and for a couple of seconds I dream of swimming in manic circles, but the rest is a black and white blur. Dr. Thorsteinsdottir, the therapist on the fourth floor I see every Tuesday during my lunch hour, says depressed people don't remember their dreams as often as happy people, which depresses me. I'd be happy if I could remember any small part of just one dream.

The next morning, on my way to the hospital, after sleeping two hours, I stop at Ma's like I do every morning. For breakfast. She usually cooks me four strips of bacon and three eggs fried in bacon grease, a bowl of grits with extra salt and extra butter, toast with raspberry jelly and honey, coffee, and a glass of pineapple juice with a splash of water.

Ma's street, Magnolia Lane, is a cul de sac shaped like a hook. All the magnolia trees were removed because of a fungus, but Ma had hers cut *before* they got sick. To be safe, she said, before they crushed her and Oscar in their sleep, even though the trees were only house-high and not big enough to hurt anything. At the beginning of the street is a nursing home I thought would be nice for Ma one day, but it's under investigation because two residents, roommates, were caught making and distributing crystal meth. Across from the nursing home is an old church that a preacher turned into a "pain management" clinic, but it was shut down and he was sent to jail for selling pills to middle-schoolers. The road is lined with ranch homes built in the 1960s, big yards and deep woods forty miles south of Nashville in this town where my parents were born, and where I have spent my life, loving it and hating it, imagining other places, going nowhere.

When I pull up, Ma is sitting at the end of her driveway, in her bathrobe, reading *The Daily Sun*. There are leaves all around her, and the wind is blowing her thin hair, but she seems perfectly content sitting there in the near-darkness reading her newspaper.

"What're you doing?" I say.

"Reading the obituaries to see if your sister made it into the paper."

I look around the neighborhood to see if anyone is watching, but it's too early, and all the nice neighbors I knew as a child are dead or gone anyway.

"I had a dizzy spell," she says. "I bent for the paper and fell right over."

Wayne Houston's house is still for sale. On the night he cut off his son's head, I stayed with Ma because she got scared with all the cop cars and media trucks and all the yellow tape. Once, from Ma's window, I saw two cops step from Wayne's house with their hands over their faces, sobbing from what they'd seen in there. All I knew about Wayne was that he'd come from Michigan to work at the GM plant. He told me this when he brought over a mac and cheese casserole after Dad died, which he said he'd made himself. After that, we only waved a few times and never had a real conversation, even after the GM plant closed last year, which I feel bad about— not talking to him. I suppose his wife moved back to Michigan.

"So I decided to stay here and read the paper until someone showed up."

Across the street, a skeleton has fallen on its face, half-buried in wet leaves. The yard next to it holds a deflated ghost. Both porches hold rotting jack-o-lanterns.

Just then, Dr. Wright comes up behind me carrying a walking stick shaped like a scythe.

"A woman was raped in the Target parking lot," Ma says. "I never have liked Target."

"I'll tell you who has the best-looking place on the street," Dr. Wright says. "It's that black family down at the end who moved in last month. They keep a good-looking place."

"That's a very offensive—last month?" I wonder how long Dr. Wright has been making house calls.

"Would anyone like to help me up?" Ma says.

"It was the last of September," Wright says. "Just after I married your mother."

"I've read every obituary twice. I don't see your sister. I wonder what picture she'd want to use, anyway. She's always hated getting her picture made. Never once smiled that I remember."

"Are you having chest pains?" Dr. Wright says.

"No, but my ass is numb."

"I'm referring to Benjamin. He looks a little woozy and he's holding his heart."

It's true. I'm woozy and I'm holding my heart. I don't know how I missed Dr. Wright having married my mother. Maybe he goes for long walks every morning while I eat breakfast. Maybe he sleeps late. Or leaves early. Dr. Thorsteinsdottir says depressed people often lose their powers of observation. She says if I noticed how miserable others are, I'd feel better. She says I should ask others about *their* suffering. Mostly, she says, I should start asking myself better questions about myself, but I'm not sure where to start.

"Let's get you inside," Dr. Wright says.

"I'm ready," Ma says.

He grabs my elbow and guides me slowly up the driveway, using his walking stick, telling me *nice and easy now, everything's going to be fine.*

Behind us, Ma says, "Another baby was found in the Duck River inside a garbage bag. Third one this year."

Dr. Wright sits me at the kitchen table, brings me a paper bag and tells me to breathe into it while he goes back for Ma. I want to go to work and tell Bruce what's going on. But it's Monday, so he'll only want to talk about how he spent the weekend helping his one-footed wife meet the new challenges she set for herself, which I already heard all about on Friday: hikes, karate lessons, kickball games, a waltz, etc.

Then I think of calling my daughter, Kimberly, in Tokyo, who is eighteen now. Just so she'll remember me, her father. Maybe she would say, "I love you." The last time I talked to her, many months ago, she said she was afraid to touch the same phone her stepfather, Dr. Maleszewski, touched. I invited her then to come live with me, but she said my sighs hurt her ears, and Ma's house hurt her nose, and the town hurt her eyes, and the only place where she felt safe was in her own bedroom closet, which she had trouble leaving, which is my fault. I'm afraid she inherited my genes for being strange and large and lonely. I would visit her, but I'm afraid of flying. I've never been on a plane. No way could I remain in the air all the way to Tokyo. I'd like to hear her voice now, but the time difference makes it too early there anyway, a mistake I've made before, which Kimberly scolded me for by saying, "You forgot the time difference, Daddy-doofus. Now you've woken up *my parents*." Doofus was one of her first words, learned from her mother. A year later, she put Daddy in front of Doofus, and continues to do so, insisting it's an endearment.

Dr. Wright comes in with Ma, both of them giggling.

She says, "You want some breakfast, Benny?"

I answer.

"Move that bag away from your mouth, honey."

"Yes ma'am, please."

"You know what Anthony eats for breakfast? Bran cereal with a prune. Then he poops at six a.m. like clockwork."

"And now," he says, "I'm off to the Y for my 1K swim, 3K run, and 5K bike ride. I'm behind schedule after being up so late. The globe is off its axis. But I'll be on the battlefield by two."

"Isn't he amazing?" Ma says. "After all that exercise, he does his service-work. He walks around Franklin and talks to dead soldiers."

"*They* talk to *me*, dear. They cry, and I console. All six thousand two hundred and fifty-two of them." He kisses Ma on the lips, pats my head and literally whistles Dixie on his way out the door.

"Isn't he cute?" Ma says. "The last of a dying breed, that man. So chivalrous." Then she whistles the same tune while measuring her grits.

"Why wasn't I informed of your marriage?"

"It wasn't a secret, Benny."

"But why did you have to marry him?"

"On our first date he listened to my heart and said my arthritis was verging on critical, so he recommended moving in. I said we'd have to get married first under the eyes of God, then he put a handkerchief on the ground and proposed on bended knee. It's nice to have a man around the house. Isn't he handsome? And such bedside manner. Such a soft touch."

"Could I have some bourbon?"

She squeezes the orange bulb of a medicine dropper over my coffee until a drop of bourbon comes out. She does the same for hers. This is what Dad had done for both of them every morning of their married lives for forty years until the day he went to work and removed a patient's leg instead of her appendix. A day later, after the patient continued to complain about the missing leg *and* the persisting appendix pain, Dad carried a lethal dose of sodium pentothal to his Cadillac, which he'd mistakenly parked in the reserved space of the CEO, Mr. Saviano, and injected himself.

When I get to my desk, I see Bruce has called in sick. I call his cell immediately to tell him all about my night and my morning. His wife picks up. She says, "Listen. You call my husband again and I'll march very quickly to wherever you are and personally stomp your fat ass until you bleed to death, is that clear?" She hangs up before I can answer. I wonder what Bruce has told her. The truth? That he'd rather be with me, except that he doesn't have the courage? The fluorescent lights spin around my eyes while a distant phone rings. Then a man runs in screaming, covered in burns after setting a bee-hive on fire, which he did for revenge, he tells me, after suffering a sting. Then a boy comes in staring at a small computer he's carrying, earplugs in, a thin nail stuck between his eyes which his mother says his father put there with a nail gun from across the room (which means extra paperwork for me), then a failed overdoser, then a baby with a blood-soaked diaper, then an Amish kid by ambulance—maybe a broken neck after a truckdriver creamed his horse (dead) and buggy (totaled) on the Columbia Pike, plus a broken foot caused by the EMT who slammed the ambulance doors too quickly—then the guy in the chicken suit who waves outside Fred's Chicken Palace limps in carrying his chicken head, the feathers around his right thigh bloody from a passing gunshot, then a priest suffering chest pains confesses to me that he has done unspeakable things and asks me to hold his hand while I call another priest he knows (long-distance) who administers last rites too loudly over the phone's intercom, then Dr. Thorsteinsdottir, my own counselor from the fourth floor, suffers a seizure while listening to a patient and gets admitted at once, nonresponsive, which means I'll miss tomorrow's appointment. And between all these cases is the normal and constant onslaught of the sick and flu-ridden and fevered battalion of doubled-over people who vomit into disposable cups and cough into my face while I ask them to repeat the spellings of their names and their home addresses and verify their insurance (no one ever asks how *I'm* doing) until, at 9 p.m., I go home and fall into bed, feeling sick myself, too tired to eat anything but the box of cherry-filled chocolate-topped Krispy Kremes I pick up on the way home, which puts me right to sleep.

Ma calls at midnight.

"It's louder tonight, Benny—that awful-pretty, terrible-sad singing. Come listen."

I ask her why Dr. Wright, her "man around the house," can't take care of it.

"Take off your mask, honey."

I remove my mask and repeat my question.

"He won't wake up, Benny. You should look at him too, while you're here. I'm scared. And your sister's still not answering her phone. We're very upset."

I'm pretty sure I have a fever. But I get up anyway, grab my broom handle and flashlight, put a coat on over the robe I put on over my pajamas, find my slippers and slip them on. When I get to my car, I see that all four of my tires are missing. My car (Dad's old Cadillac) is up on blocks, and the wheels are gone. I'm sure, at this moment, if the entire gang of hoodlums stepped forward, I would use my broomstick to bludgeon them to death. But no one is around. All the lights in all the apartments are out. So I walk. I walk through the field between the complex and the car wash, through the center stall, then go uphill behind the nursing home to get to Magnolia Lane, certain my fever is nearing 102.

Ma's door key doesn't work. I knock and ring the bell and knock and ring the bell and knock and ring the bell.

"Who is it?" Ma says.

"It's me, Ma. Why did you change the locks?"

"Is that you, Benny?"

"It's me, Ma."

She lets me in. She says, "Anthony changed the locks to keep out the carpet-baggers. He's in the bedroom. Did you bring your stethoscope?"

I find Dr. Wright lying completely naked, open eyes pointed toward the ceiling. His erect penis also points toward the ceiling. Ma stands behind me, leaning her head on my back. Through her bedroom window, I hear, for the first time, a strange and beautiful voice singing in what seems like a foreign language.

"Did I kill him, Benny? He said he'd taken an extra vitamin, then he applied some ointment to his plunger and asked me to sit on top of him so he could apply it, and it felt pretty good, Benny, I'm not ashamed to tell you—so maybe I got carried away and killed him. And listen to that singing. I know you hear it."

"I hear it. I'll take a look."

"You should examine Anthony first, Benny. Anthony should have priority."

"I'll get to him as soon as I can," I say.

She starts crying. She says, "He'll be right back, Anthony. He has to see about the voice first, then he'll see you."

The voice is a loud single-note wail that might be some European word for "help." Or either it's not a word at all. I go through the back yard and step into the woods, duck beneath low limbs, step over fallen limbs, push through vines. I shine my light in front of me and stop once to knock away a spider's web stretched between branches. A sweatball pops through my forehead—I'm in no shape for a hike—and I start breathing through my mouth. The air is cold enough to burn my lungs a little, but I continue toward the voice, which circles my head and retreats and comes back. I feel my way in a zig-zaggy pattern, holding my broomstick (which I can't even see) in front of my face.

The voice sounds like it's singing of terrible things it doesn't know the words for. I step over a limb and lose a slipper. This is a voice that has seen more blood than me. A dizzy spell hits me so hard I have to lean against a tree. The voice sounds like a child is crying at the same pitch that an old woman is wailing. I lift my bare foot. I picture faces on fire. The tree I'm leaning against is too thin. The voice is holding a note now that is being sustained longer than seems possible for any human. I lower my bare foot to the cold ground. I picture the voice bubbling up from some primitive pool of lava a few thousand miles below me. It's painful and playful and heartbreaking and honest and ancient and new, intended for no audience. The voice knocks something loose between my throat and chest. It swipes the dust off my eyes and squeezes my tear ducts. I hold steady to my tree, suddenly very weak, ready to sob like I haven't sobbed since—since I don't know when.

When I lift my light, I see an abandoned car nearly swallowed-up with weeds. The voice, very clearly, is coming from inside the car. It stops.

"Benny?"

I don't answer.

"You're breathing hard, Benny. Is your asthma acting up?"

I shine the light toward the back window and see my sister's face.

"What're you doing in there?" I say.

"What's it sound like? You should sit down before you have a heart attack."

It sounds like a good idea. I step through some high weeds, put my broomstick under my arm and tug on the driver's side door, which opens on my third pull. I fall behind the wheel, rest my bare foot on the gas pedal, close the door and exhale.

Penny says, "Turn off that light."

I do. I stare through the dark windshield. I say, "Your singing was—I can't believe that was you. So much better than any of your recitals."

"How would you know?"

She has a point. I never went to any of her recitals. In fact, I'm not sure, before tonight, that I've ever heard her sing. She's fifteen years younger—Ma calls her "my accident." She was three when I went to college, seven when I got married, fifteen when Dad killed himself. There are large sections of her life I know nothing about. I do know that everyone praised her singing while she grew up, promised her a brilliant future. She attended Belmont on a scholarship, dropped out when the teachers criticized her, transferred to a state school, changed majors, dropped out again, had a brief visit to a psychiatric ward, married a man she met in rehab, divorced, returned to rehab, lived with other men, lost jobs, lived on credit cards. Most of this, I learned from her voice messages.

She says, "Wayne used to bring me out here. Before he did what he did. We used to hang out in the back seat."

"Hang out?"

"Have sex, Benjamin. Get loaded and have sex. *She* cheated on him first though, which is what no one knows. He wanted her to take their son back to Michigan so we could be together. He was such a good listener."

"Did he ever mention me?"

She sighs at this. I picture her eyes rolling. "Why would he mention *you*? He was a good listener, Benny. He was interested in *me*. But you think you know somebody, you know? I guess you can never really know anyone very well for sure, can you?"

There's something accusatory in her tone, but I don't respond. She starts humming. The humming is peaceful and melodic and more soulful than any humming I've ever heard.

"Dad's favorite," I say.

She stops.

I say, "Do you feel like singing it?"

On the first note to "Ave Maria," my hands fall from the wheel and I close my eyes and see a different shade of darkness that makes me dizzy with how light I feel inside of it. It's the same dizziness that hits me when I imagine Kimberly stepping straight from her Tokyo closet into my well-lit living room, smiling.

When she finishes, I open my eyes. I wipe my cheeks. I say, "Wow. That was really—I really, I don't know why I'm so—I'm not feeling too—"

"Did you know our mother lost her marbles and married Dr. Wright?"

I wipe my eyes again. I take a deep breath. I say, "How did *you* know?"

"I've been living next door. Wayne gave me a key the night before he did what he did. His wife kept a well-stocked pantry, I'll give her that—lots of beans. Ma couldn't live in sin, of course, and I see Dr. Wright leave every morning before dawn, then I see you show up to stuff your face after that. I haven't slept in a very long time."

"I didn't know."

"You're not very observant."

I look through the windshield, then out the window. "It's peaceful out here."

"It's the only place that makes sense. I never want to be out there again around all those people who will be staring at me because I was involved with Wayne. Everyone knows we were sleeping together. I know they know. I can't go back out there."

"I can't either. I'm having a—"

"And now Ma's lost her mind and married Dr. Wright, who's crazy too. Don't you think Dr. Wright's crazy?"

"Yes, but he's dead. He's lying in Ma's bed right now, dead as a post."

"What?"

"Stiff as a board."

"What?"

"Dead as a dead cat."

She pauses. I picture her mouth hanging open. "Did you call anyone?"

I don't answer.

"Christ, Benny. You left Ma alone with Dr. Wright's dead body in her bed? Are you serious? What the fuck is wrong with you?"

I'm not sure how to answer this. I start humming. I hum Ave Maria, but it sounds ugly, even to my ears.

"Do you ever ask yourself why your wife left you or why your daughter hates you? Do you ever ask yourself why you'll always be alone? You make my stomach hurt."

She reaches over the seat, grabs my flashlight, then takes off through the woods, straight toward Wayne's back door. It's just like her to steal my flashlight and leave me stranded.

There are no crickets, no tree frogs, no owls, no little feet scurrying, no wind to clang the leaves, no leaves, no streetlights, no traffic noise, no crackling from a power line, no moon, not a single sound or light from the whole dead neighborhood.

Penny's singing voice rises inside my head again and stays. It swirls around and swells. It pushes its feet against one ear and its hands against the other ear. It burrows, climbs, crawls, stomps, and whispers. It claws the backs of my eyes. It drops a jackhammer, apologizes, winks, glues a teacup, screams the color orange. It builds a house of dynamite on a cloud that sits on the ocean and asks sweetly, please, to be tucked in. Then pauses. Then mocks the sound of ticking. Then sings again, more softly.

I grip the steering wheel. I push the accelerator. I stick my head out the window and shout as loudly as my puny voice will let me. I say, "I'm coming, Ma. I'll be right there, Ma!" I will make the calls for her. I'll spend the night with her. I will fix her breakfast. I'll move in. I'll be good.

A Serious Question

Charlotte Blanchard rushed to her ringing phone carrying the last bag of kitty poop she ever intended to carry (having returned her two cats to the shelter that very morning) and held the poop beside her while she listened to her dying friend, Brother Michael, of St. Francis of Assisi Parish (Milton, Ga.), apologize for disturbing her on such a beautiful Saturday morning. Her "hello" must have sounded short-winded and resentful because he got to the point straightaway: he wondered whether she might spare some time to grant him a final favor.

Her thoughts chased themselves like this: (1) How much time, exactly (2) selfish bitch (3) my actions will be rewarded (4) previous thought = selfishness (5) everything in this short life, save pending death, is petty (6) don't plop kitty-poop on table (7) the all-seeing eyes of the Almighty are watching how I treat His dying servant (8) a goddamned flea from Brother Michael's mutt is biting my ankle (9) it's the duty of the living to console the sick and dying (10) I'm pleased he thought enough of me to be the one he chose to call (11) previous thought = vanity (12) shouldn't it make me happy to help someone needing help (13) it will help the one needing help, which is more important. (14) Starting when, exactly?

Brother Michael was eighty, hobbled with chronic pain, lungs and heart doomed to fail within a year. He was Charlotte's best (only?) friend, as well as a second cousin she'd met three years earlier when she retired to coastal Georgia, having moved at 65 from a large city in the far north, eager to flee snow and shed coats and cold co-workers and three ex-husbands. On Sunday nights, he occupied her sofa too long, feeling lonely, sipping her not-so-inexpensive wine, nibbling on peaches she sliced for him because his teeth were gone, asking for refills while they traded confessions—his gambling habits for her increasingly agnostic and anti-social attitudes—until she grew tired and wanted to be alone again, at which point she'd hand him his cane and open the door and say, "You're absolved! Go in peace!"

"What I need," Michael said now, "is a ride to Walmart."

"No," she said. "Absolutely not." She pictured the congested aisles bursting to the seams with Saturday-morning mobs of the great unwashed clamoring for life-saving bargains, and her stomach produced a violent reaction. She looked at her kitchen floor (ball of cat hair in the corner), due for its daily sweeping and weekly mopping.

"No," she repeated. "I'd have an anxiety attack before we found a parking space." She looked through her spotty kitchen window at the flowerbed that needed weeding and the azaleas that needed watering. "Ask me something else."

"Some anonymous soul left two hundred dollars in the collection basket last week with a note requesting the money be used for a rectory vacuum cleaner. You know anything about that?"

The rectory hadn't seen a vacuum in forty years and desperately needed one, but she never intended to get involved in the shopping or delivering of the damned thing. But here was the old truism at work—punishment for another good deed.

He said, "We could find a cheap one and have enough left for some scratch-offs and a bus ticket."

"I am *not* going to Walmart," Charlotte said. "Who needs a bus ticket?"

"The new brother is here, some kid from Cleveland who wears a backwards Yankees cap. They've already given him my truck, Charlotte, which he's already using to pick up some things he wants to install in my room—*his* room. Father Bob is eager to see me leave."

He'd talked of this day coming, but Charlotte had lost track of the date. He'd been instructed to take a bus to a church-owned home in Indiana where he would live out his final days. Charlotte sensed he had a more serious question on his mind. She feared he was gearing up to ask whether he could move into her guest bedroom.

He said, "Helen has made some messes I need to clean up before I leave."

Helen was the blind/deaf mutt he'd rescued from the shelter a year ago, the same day the doctors had issued Michael's death sentence. From the shelter, he'd taken her straight to Charlotte's house, quite proud of himself for being her hero, oblivious to the dog's skin condition (bald spot on its rump) and its profound odor. When he set Helen on the floor, she spun in manic circles, bumped into a table leg, barked at the table, spun rapidly a few more times and then passed out, briefly, collapsing nose-first. Charlotte's two cats immediately hissed and howled and protested so violently that within three minutes Charlotte said, "Take her away." So he did, but not before a flea jumped from Helen and burrowed into Charlotte's carpet to deposit a first generation of eggs. She battled the infestation for months afterward at considerable expense, and each time a cat scratched herself, she cursed Michael and his mutt. The fleas were the clincher in her decision to return the cats. This afternoon, she planned to wrap up her dishes and flea-bomb every room. After that chore, she would not waste another minute tending to any animal or any animal-related problem ever again.

Michael said, "I suppose I have no alternative but to catch that bus." He paused as if to see whether Charlotte would introduce an alternative. He said, "Would you want to give me a ride to the station?"

"Okay," she said, a little too quickly. "I could do that."

"Can we go to Walmart first?"

"No."

"It'll be a pilgrimage. I'll bet you ten bucks we learn something valuable."

"Give me a break."

"Wouldn't you feel guilty refusing a dying man—your second cousin, no-less—his final wish on this earth?"

"Going to Walmart is your final wish? That's pathetic."

"I have to get my house in order. Surely you of all people—"

"Shit." She plopped her bag of kitty poop on the table. Her stomach made a noise. She closed her eyes. She said, "Give me an hour to prepare myself."

At this morning's breakfast, Father Bob lowered his paperback book of jokes to remind Michael that he needed to vacate his room by the end of the day so the new brother, "a handsome young scholar from Cleveland," could move in. Then Father Bob dipped his spoon into his oatmeal and lifted his book again, leaving Michael to face his hard-boiled egg.

He dreaded, with every ounce of his dying soul, going to "the home" in Indiana where The Church sent dying men like him to live (he was fairly sure of this) among a few criminal clergy who were paid (unlike him) to retire there. The home had a no-pet rule. He imagined neck-deep snow, marrow-freezing cold, no trees, no flowers, no birds. When he bought his daily scratch-offs, it was with the honest intention of donating his winnings to the home so they could spruce up the place, make it easier for its inhabitants to approach their deaths.

After breakfast, he called Charlotte on the kitchen phone so Father Bob wouldn't hear. While they talked, he stared out the back door at the live oak sprawling through the adjacent park, limbs crawling along the ground, a bronze plaque planted beside it like a tombstone. What he wanted was to ask Charlotte if he and Helen could move into her guest bedroom at the opposite end of her house, complete with its own bathroom. But he knew it was a long shot. Last Sunday, when he brought her a basket of peaches and told her about the sign in front of the peach stand ("Nobody retires and moves up north") she'd amended it, saying "*Almost* nobody." On the phone now, he started with a simple question. He asked for a ride to Walmart.

"No," she said. "Absolutely not."

He decided he'd ask about the guest bedroom later, once her mood had softened.

She would have to tell him "No." She meant for her house to be empty of living things that made noise or produced waste or required attention of any kind. She meant to be more ruthless, finally, in finding the peace she assumed retirement would deliver. Lately, she wondered whether working twenty years as Public Health Director of a crowded and troubled county had given her a peace-acquisition disorder. Sometimes, during her nightly bouts of insomnia, she composed her own obituary: "Charlotte Blanchard wasted her life and ruined her retirement by working sixty hour weeks, nights/weekends, cultivating the habit of worry. She wasted each day managing the damage bred from others' bad decisions, losing sleep each night to waking dreams of catastrophic outcomes, was greeted each morning by reports announcing new bad news that required day-long meetings inside airless rooms attended by dead-eyed workers drowning in defeat. She argued with her own idiot bosses over ways to educate citizens and deliver services with increasingly decimated budgets, though occasionally Ms. Blanchard *did* leave the building to battle myopic bureaucrats, likewise getting nowhere ('bang head here' said the poster on her former best friend's wall). She also failed to find peace in her hour-long train commute inside a sea of slow-dying faces, nor did she find peace at home through a series of three husbands (one per seven years, on average) who were each given notice because they needed their own problems nursed before they could lift an occasional hand to procure or prepare fresh vegetables or to help maintain (yet alone *improve*) a house that continued to depreciate inside a neighborhood that continued to decline once the publicly approved tax-funded football stadium moved in, delivering drunks who urinated, vomited, and defecated in her untrimmed hedges."

In retirement, she planned to worry over no one. Except Ruby, her only child, who worked in the London music industry, which meant she lived with a series of musicians who took advantage of her. Charlotte had pushed Ruby to pursue her own ambitions, to stop letting others (especially men) dictate the terms on which she lived her life. Ruby resented this concern, and three months ago, when Charlotte reminded her to use clean needles and covered penises (if she needed them at all), Ruby exploded with a profanity-laced tantrum, calling Charlotte a hyper-critical self-righteous bully who knew what was best for everyone but herself. Charlotte told her forty-year-old daughter to call her when she decided to become an adult. When Charlotte called a week later, Ruby's line was disconnected. In the meantime, Charlotte worried over no one else. Her long-suffering parents were finally dead (though she worried she hadn't done enough for them), and when her only brother, a tobacco-company lobbyist, claimed "Obamacare" was "evil socialism," she hung up on him and planned never to speak to him again. The only person Charlotte missed was her ex-best friend and co-worker, Kim, who told Charlotte in an email just before she moved that, for the sake of her sanity, she was "excising perniciously toxic people" from her life. Charlotte replied, asking "Who the hell is perniciously toxic? Me? Do you mean *me*? How could you mean *me*? I got you hired and promoted, you ungrateful wench." Charlotte wrote right back, apologized for lashing out, admitted to be heartbroken and confused.

So she retired, alone, telling herself all she needed was to be free from talking to people who talked only of their own problems. All she needed, she said, was to be free of people. She sat outside her ocean-side bungalow and stared at the sunrises and grew a little better, slowly, at finding peace. All she needed was to eliminate further worry, action she took this morning when she returned her cats, whose body-waste, vomit, hair, fleas, and special needs demanded too much attention.

On the phone now, Michael said, "Charlotte, I have a serious question for you."

She squinted through the window at her dry hydrangeas and steadied her resolve.

"But I'll wait," he said. "So you can tell me no while you look me in the eye."

"Okay," she said. "If that's what you want."

Michael leaned against the oak tree, telling it goodbye. There were no trees like this in Indiana. In Indiana—at least the part they were sending him to—there was corn. When there wasn't corn, there were snow-covered cornfields. This tree, however, was something people made a point to visit. Tourists petted it, posed for pictures. It had survived hurricanes, droughts, floods, a Civil War skirmish. The plaque said, "This old oak, dating to the 12th Century, has served as a meeting place for lovers since Indian times."

It still attracted lovers. On three occasions over the years— when Michael was a better walker and ventured out on insomnia-fighting strolls—his late-night footsteps sent people scurrying while they pulled up their pants. Each time, he yelled for them to come back and enjoy a night beneath the tree while they were young. But they always kept running.

He'd arranged his first meeting with Charlotte here, hoping the tree would make her feel better about moving to a faraway place where she knew no one. But it had been a hot summer day and she'd batted mosquitoes while she cynically read the plaque, and she never really saw the tree at all. She said, "How many Indian men do you suppose were murdered on the roots by white men?" She said, "How many of these limbs have held a noose?"

Now, to rest his legs, he sat on one of the low limbs held off the ground by a series of bricks. He placed his hand on her bark, looked over his head at the tapestry of Spanish moss and thanked the tree for being such a strong and steady presence. He thanked her for providing awe and wonder for 900 years. He told her to hang in there for another century or two. He dabbed his eye. He sniffed and called himself a silly old dying fool. From somewhere above and behind, he heard a woman's voice.

Charlotte took a shower, applied makeup and dressed in the white slacks and scarlet blouse she knew would most comfortably hide the fifteen pounds she'd added since retirement—nice clothes that would easily separate her from the trash-dressing Walmart herd. In her pocket, she stuffed a packet of sani-wipes to use on the cart she'd have to touch.

Father Bob answered the rectory door with his dour face, peered over his glasses, and lifted his unkempt eyebrows into question marks, remaining mute, as if to demonstrate that Charlotte could never threaten a holy man's vow of silence. His eyes were slate-gray, blank as ocean foam. She wanted to yell, HELLO, IT'S CHARLOTTE, YOUR EUCHARISTIC MINISTER WHO SHARES THE ALTAR WITH YOU EVERY SUNDAY AT 8:30 MASS, DISHING OUT THE BODY OF CHRIST? She knew he didn't approve of this—a woman standing before the altar in the second decade of the twenty-first century, for God's sake. The fact that this bothered him was the only reason she went to church. It occurred to her now to remove her wide-brimmed gardening hat and big sunglasses. He didn't change expressions, but he did step aside and wave her across the threshold with his book. The rectory odors assaulted her at once. Helen's mess swirled in the stale air amidst the dust, the dankness, and the mold of the dark house, layers of stink piled among the odors of old men who could no longer smell themselves.

He said, "Could I ask you a serious question?"

"Please," Charlotte said.

He lifted his paperback, cleared his throat, and started reading. "These three brothers went weekly to the same bar for many years. Then two of the brothers moved away. The brother who stayed behind kept visiting the bar, each time ordering three beers, telling the bartender that one was for each of his long-gone brothers and one was for himself. A month later, however, he came in and ordered only two beers. The bartender said, 'I'm so sorry for your loss.' The brother said, 'What loss? I quit drinking.'"

Father Bob looked over his book to Charlotte. He said, "Is that funny? Isn't that a good, you know, a fine—"

"Do you have anything about facing death? Facing death alone? Finding the courage to face death after you've been kicked out of your home? Anything like that?"

"Would you excuse me?" He walked back into the dark bowels of the rectory.

Charlotte knocked on Brother Michael's door and got no response. She called loudly for him and got no reply. She even called for Helen, got the same result.

The voice said, "Hey! Let's get a move on for Christ's sake!"

Michael turned to see Charlotte in the rectory's back yard, hands on hips, grimacing from the heat. He made his way to her as quickly as he could, found her in the kitchen some minutes later holding an empty water glass, frowning.

He said, "Let's tell Helen we're leaving." He found Helen lying on his bed, the cloudy-white orbs of her red-rimmed eyes half-hidden beneath her bushy bangs. When he put his hand to her nose, she wagged her tail, jumped up and spun around six times, then fell over like she'd been shot.

"She still passes out like that," he said. "After she gets excited and spins. Then she bounces right back up. I think the Holy Ghost overtakes her."

They stared at Helen's limp body. In a couple of seconds, she bounced up, barked at the window, then scratched her face.

"She still has fleas?" Charlotte said. "And she sleeps with you?"

"Ever since I took her to your house, she's had fleas. You should look into that. Daddy will be back soon," he told the dog. "Don't make a mess."

"She's deaf, Michael."

"She's such a good listener that I forget."

Charlotte opened the front door, motioning Michael ahead, but he had to remove his Braves cap from the hat rack and pull it snug. She held his cane and sighed while he checked himself in the foyer mirror and finally stepped back into the Hades-like heat of the south Georgia August, squinting against the brightness.

"Can we raise the top?" he said. "The wind gets in my ears and I can't hear too well."

"No. Let's air you out a bit."

She sped through downtown, accelerating beneath three yellow lights, creating such a breeze that Michael had to hold his cap on his head.

"I have a serious question for you," he said.

"I can't hear you," Charlotte answered. "Too much wind."

The Walmart parking lot was packed, of course, a lot the size of a great lake reflecting the heat back at them. All the trucks and SUVS held bumper stickers campaigning for Jesus. Some rear windshields held numbers that revealed affiliations with NASCAR, the "sport" most attractive to the sort of person Charlotte liked least: beer-chugging, blood-thirsty apes too similar to her second husband. The loud, gas-guzzling, space-hoarding vehicles were driven by extra-salty primates eager to fill them with plastic crap they'd take back to trailers moored in multi-generational swamps preserved by people who continued to vote Republican, a behavior she found as baffling as being a chicken who prayed to Colonel Sanders. Presently, she was stalled behind an obesity parade: an obese couple and their seven obese kids waddling along in T-shirts that featured the faces of professional wrestlers. Two children spat in opposite directions. She placed her palm over the center of the steering wheel, prepared to push her horn and hold it.

"Easy does it," Brother Michael said. "No need to run over anyone."

It was easier to feel forgiving from her home by the ocean. She pictured the two palm trees in her back yard and the spot between them which offered a breeze-filled unobstructed view all the way to the horizon. She noticed then that the obese man had a prosthetic leg, and he was calling out for his family to slow down, but they'd already abandoned him.

Brother Michael pulled a handicapped parking tag from his jacket pocket and hung it on Charlotte's mirror. He said, "I've left this to you in my will. My most valuable possession except for Helen. And my shoes."

She pulled into a handicapped space, which still seemed a half-mile from the entrance.

"Did you see my shoes?" he said.

"I saw them." Last month, Charlotte put a hundred-dollar bill in the collection basket wrapped in an anonymous note requesting the money be spent on new shoes for Michael because the soles of his old shoes had flapped too loudly for too long, making ungodly noises all over the church, disturbing the living and the dead. That same night, he dropped by to show her the brogans he'd found on sale for $39.95, paid for, he said, by a secret admirer. Then he confessed to spending sixty dollars on lottery tickets.

Charlotte said, "If we leave the top down, your tag will be gone when we get back."

"Where's your faith in humanity, Charlotte? I'll bet you ten bucks it'll still be here."

She left it down, silently rehearsing an *I told you so*. As they ambled toward the door, Charlotte slowing to half-steps, an old lady in a wheelchair zoomed past, dangerously close to running over Charlotte's foot. The lady wore a loose tank-top that revealed tattoos of three crosses—one on the back of her neck and one atop each shoulder.

"Looks like the lame will enter first," Charlotte said.

"I'm right behind you," Michael answered.

By the time Charlotte watched three big women secure their belongings inside their suitcase-size purses and tuck them into their carts and launch their journeys, and by the time she had coated her own cart's handle with a sani-wipe, Michael had zoomed away in a motorized cart and raced toward the farthest aisle. Charlotte hurried after him (without removing her sunglasses and hat), worried they'd get separated and she'd get lost. Ahead of him, the wheelchaired-woman turned abruptly toward the lingerie, and Michael collided with her.

"Whiplash!" he shouted. He grabbed the back of his neck and giggled.

The woman's eyes narrowed into black coals. She said, "If I could get out of this chair, I'd whip your ass."

Charlotte stepped between them to intervene, if need be, though her stomach churned audibly at the thought. The woman's curls were wild and wavy, which somehow pointed to the abundant wrinkles on her cheeks and made Charlotte's eyes go to her beefy shoulders and flexed arms and black-gloved hands that tightly gripped her wheels.

"I had the right-of-way, ma'am," Michael said. "You failed to give a signal."

The woman looked at Charlotte. She said, "You need to keep your daddy on a goddamned leash or either take him back to the nursing home before he fucking kills somebody or gets hisself killed one." In her coal-colored eyes, Charlotte saw the history of bitterness she'd collected. She shot Charlotte another stare, then pushed herself toward the negligees. A bubble of rage hatched in Charlotte's stomach and turned hot inside her chest. She shouted, "Heal thyself, inbred swine." Then she rushed to catch Michael, already way ahead of her.

"Ha," he said over his shoulder. "She thought I was young enough to be your father."

"I have to go home now," Charlotte said. But Michael kept moving, rounding the corner farthest from the entrance. He veered around a large woman in a navel-exposing tank-top whose entire face, except for her right eye, was covered in bandages. Her cart held six gallons of bleach and a case of Coke. When her sharp blue eye caught Charlotte's eye, Charlotte looked away, but the woman's gaze delivered a piercing stab Charlotte interpreted as this: "You think you know my life-story because my face is wrapped in bandages, bitch?"

Michael looked over his shoulder again. He said, "I *had* the right of way."

They waded through a congregation of loud men wearing camouflaged caps, shirts and pants. The smell of cigarettes and body odor assaulted Charlotte so violently she covered her nose.

Behind her, someone sneezed. A loud maniac laughed at his own punchline, which, if she deciphered correctly, was this: "Shit— shot the motherfucker three times square in the goddamned neck before he fucking fell brother." The diction itself caused her great distress. She didn't mean the regional dialect, which she found refreshingly musical and colorful in the right mouths at the right moments; it was the manner in which this man's vowels and consonants swirled in a mush-mouthed blender before they fell from lazy lips, Neanderthal language similar to the cockney employed by her first husband's tribe, for example.

Brother Michael stopped suddenly and said, too loudly, "Pardon me, girls," to a group of hood-wearing, underwear-revealing African-American teenage boys who held their crotches while pointing through a pane of glass. They parted slowly to let Michael through, and Charlotte looked away from the violent glare that one of them shot her way. She wanted to race toward an exit and run all the way home.

Michael looked over his shoulder again. He said, "Isn't this a fascinating place?"

"I don't feel well," Charlotte said.

Parked in the center of this aisle, a teenage girl sat *inside* a cart—head tilted on a neck too weak for it, crossed eyes, mouth open to reveal cracked buck-teeth, tangled hair hanging over the back of the cart. She looked toward Charlotte and tried to smile, or so it seemed, which forced a bit of spittle to the corner of her mouth. On her lap, someone had placed a 24-roll case of toilet paper. Charlotte looked down the aisles on both sides of the girl, saw no sign of a guardian.

"Dear God," she said. "It's a literal basket case."

"Are you talking to me?" Michael said, and he accelerated quickly, which made Charlotte walk faster than she wanted to. When she caught up with him, he'd turned into the vacuum aisle, where a very pregnant girl of about fourteen examined her choices while a topless child in diapers sat on the ground behind her, putting something in its mouth.

"Dirt Devil," Brother Michael said. "I like the sound of that."

The pregnant mother chewed her thumbnail while she inspected a vacuum.

Brother Michael looked at Charlotte. He said, "Can I ask you something?"

The mother's thumb went deeper into her mouth, her lips closed around it, and her cheeks imploded, clearly bewildered by the difficult choice she needed to make this very moment with help from no one, which was the story of her doomed young life. Charlotte thought of Ruby and wondered if she was safe. What if this very second, Ruby needed her? This question sent a sharp pang to her stomach, and her stomach responded by sending a prompt signal to her lower brain informing her that if she did not immediately find a restroom, she would—

"It's a question I've been meaning to ask for awhile," Michael said.

—*shit her pants*, as the colloquial would have it.

"A delicate question," Michael said. "I'll understand if you say no."

Already, she'd reached the far late stages where she feared a single step would trigger a humiliating release. She ordered her bowels *not* to betray her here. She looked across the aisle hoping to spy a bathroom, but that aisle held only mops. She imagined a blue-vested kid (*Sam, we need a cleanup on 13 please, Sam, cleanup on 13*), cursing old people for the positions they put him in, though Charlotte was just 68 she'd explain, not old at all really, except he'd say: *Lady, if you're shitting yourself, you're either old or....*

"If you say no," Michael said, "I'll understand."

"Get up."

"What?"

She nudged his shoulder so he'd get the message and snapped her fingers three times, which made him finally start moving, though he struggled to extricate his cane. Charlotte moved onto the cart and sat, clenched tightly and raced away, one end of Michael's cane bouncing against her knee. A line of sweat broke through her forehead. She clenched and prayed to Jesus and mother Mary, who was full of grace and blessed among women who had the blessed fruit who prayed for sinners now and at the hour, she prayed.

Stupidly, she went the way they'd come, swerved to miss the teenage girl in the basket who was now turned to face her, still hugging her toilet paper, head drooped to the side, crossed eyes trying to find the object blurring by. She passed the boys with the hoods over their heads, looking like soldiers for Death who were not parting for the tattooed wheelchair-lady trying to get through from the other side, who was now equipped with a jousting rod (a flag?), and in the half-second it took to see into the lady's dark eyes, Charlotte knew she would not make it.

The cheapest Dirt Devil cost $85.22. A pregnant lady on the same aisle, whose cute child held on to her shirt, asked if she could help. The people in this town had always been quite friendly, Michael had always found. She agreed the Dirt Devil was a decent choice for the money, then she lifted the box and put it in the cart Charlotte had left behind. The kind woman even offered to push it out and load it into Michael's car, but he declined, saying he had a friend.

"The same friend who pushed you out your buggy?"

"She gets excited sometimes. But we'll be okay."

"Alrighty-then. God bless you, Father."

He did not explain, as he had many times before, that he was not a father, but a brother. In the past, he'd taken time to defend his calling, which meant explaining that he never felt called to the priesthood, a more visible position with more perks. He'd chosen the more ascetic path, vowing to keep company with people poorer than he. And for forty years (except for 1972, while campaigning for McGovern), he wandered through Mexico, Central America, South America, and the southern United States, wrestling with his own restlessness, chain-smoking, surviving dysentery, dengue fever, bacterial pneumonia, fungal meningitis, a broken back. He wandered until he reached the Georgia coast, where he admitted, finally, that he was tired. He called it home, felt afraid to leave again. But he saw no need to explain all that.

His greatest desire, at present, was to find his weak legs a seat. He held tightly to the cart and pushed it back the way they'd come. He passed the lady in the wheelchair that he'd run into and smiled as if they were old friends now, but she didn't see him. Or she ignored him. Who's to know? She looked straight ahead, inching forward with her own quiet courage.

When he rounded the corner, he saw Charlotte rushing out of the restroom, still wearing her big sunglasses and hat, face pointed down, skirting quickly along the edge of the far wall, moving in a straight line toward—the exit?

The bathroom had been full of big-bodied, loud-talking women washing hands, checking mirrors, taking their time inside the hellish wave of human waste that struck Charlotte's nostrils and snaked down her throat. She stepped around a little girl leaning against the wall, waiting, and entered the vacant handicapped stall at the end where she found a toilet already full—either unflushed or backed up—a terrible quantity and texture (spent cigarette on top), clearly the product of a poor diet. She tried to hold her breath while she locked the stall door and lowered her pants and sat (taking no time to wipe the seat) and released it all, including such prolonged and animalistic noises as she had never produced before. She covered her face with her hands and sobbed as quietly as she could.

From the next stall, the little girl said, "You ain't oppose to use the handicapped stall if you ain't handicapped."

"Shut up," Charlotte said.

"You stink." The girl flushed, then slammed her stall door.

Someone laughed. Someone said, "Tell her 'bout it, honey."

She was afraid to flush. She cleaned up quickly, as best she could, waited for a pocket of silence, then buried her underwear in the trash. She washed her hands and walked out along the edge of the furthest wall, worried over what was visible through her white slacks. She pushed up her sunglasses, pulled down her hat, stepped quickly toward the exit.

Michael saw his cane still hooked in the basket. He left his Dirt Devil where it was, got into his cart and tried to catch Charlotte in the parking lot, feeling certain that she meant to abandon him. When he got through the sliding doors, the heat snatched his breath, and the light blinded him so badly he couldn't distinguish the color of any car. He couldn't remember where she'd parked. Just ahead of him, something backed out of a space, and by the time his eyes adjusted, he knew it was her convertible, though the top was up now, the windows raised.

He stopped in the center of the row, facing her, saw her window slide down. She said, "I told you I couldn't go in there. I told you that. Are you coming?"

He parked the cart in the corral next to her car, removed his cane and fell into the passenger seat. She backed out slowly, deliberately, suddenly at odds with the panicked rush she'd been in to leave the store.

He said, "Are you okay?"

She didn't answer.

She stopped at a red light. She stared at it, saying nothing.

Michael looked at his watch.

She wanted to go home. She wanted to sit in her bathtub in her bathroom in her house. She wanted to wear her bathrobe and sip tea from her favorite cup, which held a picture of a lily, her favorite flower. She wanted to sip her tea in her favorite chair beside her favorite window, in perfect silence, perfectly alone except for her favorite cat (Sara) in her lap, purring. Then she remembered her cats were gone. She wondered then if it wouldn't be slightly comforting to have Brother Michael on the sofa beside her, sipping his own tea while he talked of something trivial.

"Let me ask you something," Michael said.

"Yes," she said. "Okay."

"I'm wondering whether you should go ahead and take me to the bus station."

She stared at the red light and did not answer.

"I have all I need: my cane, a good pair of shoes. If the anonymous person who donated $200 for a vacuum has no objections, I could buy a bus ticket. I'd even have enough left for a couple of scratch-offs."

She didn't answer. She stared at the red light.

"And would you take Helen back to the shelter? Give her another chance to get adopted? Don't worry about her mess. I've decided it would be best for Father Bob to have to deal with that. My gift to him. Green light."

She didn't answer. Behind her, someone honked.

Michael considered talking of trivial things while they rode along, but he figured Charlotte was in no mood. He was sorry he'd asked her to do something she hadn't wanted to do, which now seemed to have bothered her deeply, based on her profound silence. And now he'd burdened her with the extra chore of taking him to the bus station and taking Helen to the shelter, when all he'd wanted (he had decided while leaving the store) was to go away before he became a bigger burden.

He said, "I'm sorry your Saturday hasn't gone so well so far. Maybe it'll get better."

She pointed to her mirror. She said, "You owe me ten bucks."

"Ha. Maybe that makes us even."

The bus station was nearly empty. He'd looked at the schedule earlier, having a good idea he would end up there, so he knew his bus would be arriving soon. He could wait. He liked bus stations. He liked watching the faces that wore the important worry of leaving one place for another. On a bench outside the terminal, a middle-aged man blew cigarette smoke away from the young girl beside him who gripped a pink suitcase. This man, it was easy to see, was putting his daughter on a bus back to her mother. The girl stared at her feet, looking like she'd cried herself out before breakfast. Her father looked frustrated for not being able to say anything new that would explain the situation any better. Michael decided he would sit close to the girl so she'd feel less alone and be less scared.

He moved his cane to the ground, then swung each of his legs out slowly.

Charlotte said, "Are you sure about this? Wouldn't you rather—"

"You're absolved," he said. He gripped the door with his left hand to hoist himself up, pushed against his cane. He said, "Goodbye Charlotte. Peace be with you." He closed her door and walked away. Outside the station door, he stopped and turned, tipped his Braves cap, then stepped inside.

She let herself into the rectory, moving quietly to avoid attracting Father Bob, then entered Brother Michael's room. Helen lay on the bed, head raised, white eyes pointed up, nose twitching. Close to the pillows, two solid stools were stacked like rolls of quarters.

Helen raised her foot to scratch the side of her face. When Charlotte put her finger beneath Helen's nose, Helen chomped into it.

"Little bitch." A dab of blood pooled up on Charlotte's index finger.

Helen barked and spun six or eight quick circles, collapsed, then sprang up again, barked at the wall, scratched the other side of her face.

Charlotte fastened Helen's leash, scooped her up and carried her out, happy to honor Michael's wishes that his flea-coated, shit-covered room be left for Father Bob.

She took Helen home, placed her on the ground between her palm trees and sat beside her. Helen lifted her nose toward the ocean and swayed her head from side to side, looking like Ray Charles on his piano bench. Then Charlotte said, "Okay. Fine."

She carried Helen to the beach. She set her in the soft sand, removed her leash, and watched to see what she would do.

She ran. She ran quickly in a crooked line toward the water. Charlotte kicked off her shoes and chased her. It was tough-going in the soft sand with her tight slacks, and she was badly out of shape, but she trudged along. Already, she was breathing through her mouth. The wind lifted her hat and carried it away, but she kept going, worried Helen might disappear, or drown. Helen stopped at the water's edge, bounced backward when a wave hit her feet, then barked at the water. She barked and spun around and barked once more, now facing Charlotte.

"I'm coming," Charlotte yelled. It was low tide, and Helen was still far away.

When the next wave hit Helen's feet, she squatted and peed. She licked her lips, barked, spun three more times, and zig-zagged her way down the beach. Charlotte chased her, fell farther behind. Her thumping heart said "Stop." Helen's legs pumped so hard that she crashed and turned a perfect somersault, then bounced up like a gymnast, facing Charlotte, a pinch of wet sand clinging to her chin.

"Over here," Charlotte yelled.

Helen sprinted past her, wind blowing the hair on her face, the white orbs of her eyes wide open. Charlotte put her hands on her knees, decided to take an immediate seat in the wet sand, even in her white slacks, already stained, after all. Forty yards away, too close to the water, Helen stopped, spun eight or ten times like a maniac and passed out. A sharp pain shot down Charlotte's left arm. She put her palm on her heart and felt the pain even as she stared toward Helen, worried the next wave would drown her. Charlotte held her chest and grimaced. Helen bounced up on her own, then barked at the wave brushing across her feet.

Charlotte took a few shallow breaths and watched Helen veer toward her in a dog-drunk saunter, cocking her head left, then right, using her snout as if it were a rudder.

"What is it?" Charlotte whispered. "Are you looking for Michael?"

Helen spun three more circles, fell against Charlotte's leg and moved toward the hand Charlotte stretched her way. Helen licked her finger. Charlotte lifted her into her lap, stroked her ears, took a deeper breath and squinted over the empty ocean.

"Do you think I behaved badly? Do you think I should have brought him here so the *two* of you could make a mess of my house? Do you think we should go get him, or chase down the bus or something? What do you want from me?"

Helen lifted a paw to scratch her neck in a manic frenzy, then wiggled free and ran straight toward the water, turned three circles, peed on the foam again, barked at the air, then ran up the beach toward Charlotte's house in a determined and indirect path, propelled by her nose, knocked off course by the wind.

"Okay," Charlotte said. "Fine." She planted one knee in the wet sand and pushed herself to her feet, even as an invisible palm continued to squeeze what she assumed to be her heart. She stepped toward her house and called after Helen, pleading with her please to slow down for just one second. If she would cooperate for just one second, Charlotte would be happy to scoop her up so the two of them could go fetch Brother Michael and bring him home.

Penmanship

The moment Sister Fermina squeezed Hank Owen's hand so hard that his knuckles popped is the moment he decided he would run to his father's house in the North Carolina mountains, four hundred miles away. His father was between his third and fourth wives, so he figured it was a good time. Hank hated Sister Fermina's ninety-year-old scaly hand guiding his pencil over every curve of every letter of the alphabet, printed and cursive, lowercase and capital. He hated her office, which was a janitor's storage closet, and he hated her desk, a rotting door laid over sawhorses. He hated her sighs that came with gusts of breath that smelled like dog crap. He hated her red and yellow eyes that accused him of sins he didn't even know about. For an hour, she squeezed his hand. At the end of the hour, she shook her head and told him to go away. He intended to do just that.

That afternoon on the bus, Hank told Kerry Mendelson he was leaving. He loved her, so he wanted her to be heartbroken. He wanted her to say, "Please don't go." She held a tape player in her lap that played "Play that Funky Music," by Wild Cherry, and she was singing along in a voice that didn't sound like hers.

"I'm not coming back," Hank said.

"Listen to this part," Kerry said.

"Never," he said. "I'm *never* coming back."

"I'm working on a dance routine to this," she said. Then she played the song again.

At her stop, she patted his hand. She said, "See you next year, Hank."

"No, you won't," he said.

When he got home, he oiled his bicycle chain. He checked the south Georgia sky, cloudless, and deemed conditions worthy of takeoff. Then he called his father, Jimmy (who liked to be called by his first name), to tell him he was coming.

Jimmy said, "Hell-fire, son. I was just thinking of coming to see *you*." He started to talk again, then stopped, cleared his throat and restarted. "You never met him, but your grandfather—about a week ago, he got murdered up on Sugar Mountain." His voice was softer than Hank had ever heard it.

"These guys kidnapped him from his trailer, took him down a dirt road, stripped him naked, shot him six times in the head and left him lying in a ditch. Maybe I shouldn't be telling you this. Try not to picture it."

Hank tried not to picture his grandfather lying naked in a ditch with bullet holes in his head. Strangely, he pictured his grandfather lying on top of his father who was lying on top of him, making a bed out of each other in the same ditch.

"I'd love to see you," Jimmy said. "Jackie won't be here."

"I know. You told me—"

"She moved to Mexico with a minister she's been screwing. Try not to picture that either."

Hank had never met Jackie, his father's third wife, but they'd talked once by phone, just long enough for her to say, "He's at a bar getting shit-faced."

That night over dinner, Hank told his mother, Joan, that his father was coming the next day to pick him up.

Joan laughed. "No he's not. He'll call at the last minute and say something came up."

Henry, Hank's stepfather, said, "Maybe he means it." Then Henry sipped his milk.

Hank said, "He'll be here tomorrow at four o'clock."

"Right," Joan said. Then she and Henry argued over whether Hank should leave with his father if his father even showed up. They washed dishes, and Hank listened from the table.

Joan said, "You remember last summer when he visited and called at one a.m. asking us to bail him out of jail?"

Joan and Henry spent a lot of time reminding each other of things.

Henry said, "You remember *I* bailed him out, then took him for a beer, where he thanked me for being a good father to his son?"

Joan said, "You remember he's a salesman? And a bullshit artist?"

Hank said, "What's a bullshit artist?"

Henry said, "You remember the postcard he sent?"

Hank remembered the postcard. It was a pretty picture of the Blue Ridge mountains with handwriting on the back that looked like his.

"He should get to know his father," Henry said.

Joan dumped leftovers in the trash and didn't say anything.

Shortly after Henry and Joan got married, when Hank was five, Henry named him "Hank the leech," because Hank attached himself to Henry's leg as soon as he got home from his hardware store, then carried him through the house like that, laughing. Unlike the nuns, Henry believed Hank might one day amount to something. And just now, he seemed to be taking his side.

Henry said, "Jimmy and I had a good talk that night in the bar."

Hank said, "What's getting shit-faced?"

"He was still depressed for messing up with you. He said he'd even tried a couple times to asphyxiate himself."

"And you want me to turn my son over to him?"

Hank said, "What's a fixiate?"

Henry said, "He cried a little bit that night, feeling sorry about it all."

Joan said, "It's so typical of you to remember only the good things."

Hank said, "My grandfather was shot in the head and left naked in a ditch."

Henry said, "I remember when we didn't argue every day."

"I don't remember that," Joan said. "I don't remember why we got married." Then she broke a plate and left the pieces in the sink. Henry turned toward Hank and winked. Joan went to the porch to smoke and listen to Neil Diamond while she painted another lighthouse she would take to the gallery, where tourists snatched them up.

Henry asked Hank if he felt like working on his knuckleball, his fastball, his changeup, his slider, and his curve, a nightly ritual. Henry believed Hank would one day be a great pitcher. Or cabinet-maker. Henry said he had a good eye for strike zones and angles. He'd given Hank a tool belt and equipped him with his own eight-ounce hammer (later, he could graduate to a sixteen-ounce), a box of nails and a pile of scrap lumber and showed him proper technique in grip and form. Hank wore his tool belt now, at the kitchen table, in case something should need hammering. He took it off and got their gloves and ball and they went out into the late light of early summer, passing through the turpentine-saturated side porch where Joan finished another lighthouse and Neil Diamond said *I am, I said, to no one there.*

The next day at six, Jimmy ducked through the front door with the aura of a circus star. He wore dark glasses, and even though Hank couldn't see his eyes, he felt his father staring down at him with full approval. He was a 6' 6" giant, and he brought a gust of air into the house that smelled of something strange and new Hank would later associate with the mountains.

Jimmy said, "Hey, *pal.*"

While Jimmy and Henry talked in the kitchen, Joan pulled Hank into the living room, squatted in front of him, put her hands on his shoulders and issued a heart-to-heart.

"Look at me," she said.

He looked. Her eyes were wide and serious.

She said, "It'll only be for three weeks."

Hank had figured on staying permanently, but he thought he'd wait to tell her this by phone, three weeks from now, when she'd be used to his being gone.

She said, "I want you to call me every day and tell me how it's going. If you get homesick, let me know, and I'll be right there." She hugged him tightly.

He was pretty sure that she was crying. He was her only, and he'd never spent a single night away. She stood, wet-eyed, and walked him back into the kitchen, prepared to hand him over. When Jimmy drove off, she waved from the driveway, one hand covering her mouth, Henry beside her, one arm around her shoulders, waving with his other arm. Hank's stomach was hurting. He kept seeing his mother's wet eyes, and it made him wonder whether he should be leaving her.

Jimmy said, "You okay, pal?"

Hank said he was.

His father pointed to a spot on his shirt. When Hank looked down, Jimmy smacked him in the nose with his finger and called him a sucker.

It was 1976, and Hank was eight. Jimmy owned a custom van—carpet on the walls, floor and ceiling, a mini-refrigerator, cabinets, leather chairs, CB radio, hi-fi stereo, and a bed in the back partially concealed with a bead curtain. He told Hank to grab a couple Cokes from the fridge. Hank's mother didn't want him drinking these because she thought the sugar would make him a diabetic like his father, but here was his diabetic father telling him to get some Cokes, so he did.

Somewhere near Savannah, Hank went to the bed, where he found a stack of *Playboy* magazines. He flipped the pages slowly, not knowing what to think, except that further study was necessary. He discovered some pages that opened out to reveal a woman named in honor of a month. All the women seemed extremely comfortable lying on beds with cozy-looking blankets and pillows all around them, or sometimes even on the floor or in the back seat of a limousine without seeming embarrassed at all, really. Hank figured the people taking their pictures must have been their husbands or some family member who saw them first thing in the morning before they'd gotten dressed. They looked so comfortable that their eyes were almost shut and their mouths were open just a little like it was the most relaxed they'd ever been, like they were still half-asleep and hated the thought of getting up, which made Hank want to curl up beside them. He studied the hair between their legs and he studied their nipples and belly buttons and the curves of their hips and legs. He got to know all about them too, because in their own handwriting (much neater than his) they revealed their turn-ons and turn-offs, their hobbies, their career goals, and their definitions of perfect dates and perfect men. Most perfect dates involved flying to places like Paris or Rome in a private jet. By the time he got to the last centerfold in the last magazine, and for reasons he didn't fully understand, he began to lick the bodies on the pages. He felt a little stupid at first. Then he licked again. He found himself thinking of Kerry Mendelson, a third grader, in a whole new light. He remembered what she had confided to him about kissing her older cousin for hours at a time just so she could practice, and he suddenly wanted very badly to be the next boy she might want to practice with.

When Hank licked himself into a thirst, he went back up front, stopping at the mini-fridge for another Coke. Jimmy was listening to his CB radio, channel 19, reserved for truckers. Learning trucker language was part of Hank's education that summer. Jimmy was reading his mail, which meant he was eavesdropping without talking. He was listening for reports of Kojaks with Kodaks, or bear sightings (cop alerts) at his front door (ahead of him), especially plain wrappers (unmarked police cars) parked at specific yardsticks (mile-markers) taking pictures (using radar). Hank took his seat next to him. His father went awhile without saying anything, and then Hank realized he'd probably seen him in his rearview mirror licking his magazines. Jimmy lit a cigarette started a philosophical conversation.

He said, "You know, son, there's a lot more to a woman than just a body."

"I know," Hank said.

Jimmy said, "There's a lot more to a good relationship than just sex."

"I know," Hank said. He looked out the window at the moving woods, knowing all about it. "How much further?"

"Long way," Jimmy said.

They went awhile without talking. A few miles later, a woman's voice came over Jimmy's CB. She said, "*Silver-Lining*—is that you on 95th Street northbound over?"

"Roger that, Lady-Luck. You must be following me over?" It was a woman trucker he'd been talking to the day before when they'd both been southbound. She'd dropped a load of apples in Florida, and now she was northbound with a load of oranges.

She said, "What're *you* carrying over?"

"The fruit of my loins. My one and only from my first over."

"I don't believe you mentioned young'ns. Did you kidnap him over?"

"Got him on loan. Hey, what-say we tie on a feedbag, then tie one on, then tie each other up over?"

She laughed at this. Then she addressed Hank. She said, "Junior, I hope you get a better education than your old man got over."

Jimmy handed Hank the receiver so he could reply, but he waved it away. He knew lots of people were listening, and he didn't feel like explaining anything about his first three years at St. Francis of Assisi Catholic grade school.

"His mother tells him not to talk to strangers," Jimmy said. "But we'll get over that over."

Lady Luck and Jimmy flirted for awhile. They talked as if they thought Hank wasn't listening. Jimmy wasn't shy at all, and it made Hank want to be like him. Now, Jimmy was trying to talk Lady Luck into stopping so they could become better friends.

He said, "How 'bout a quickie at the next pickle park over?"

A pickle park was a rest area, but Hank didn't know why they called it that.

She said, "You're not that lucky, Silver Lining. I better keep her in boogie toward Virginny, where my ball and chain is waiting over."

"Hell-fire," Jimmy said. "Virginia ain't the only state for lovers over."

They talked until Jimmy took an exit and changed interstates. Lady Luck said she'd catch him in a short-short next time through. He turned off his CB and pushed in an eight-track tape of Willie Nelson, who sang about phases and stages and circles and cycles, and when that was over, he pushed in Waylon Jennings, who sang about ladies loving outlaws like babies loving stray dogs. The music made that stretch of highway look sad and lonesome. The whine of the wheels got brighter. The shadows in the woods got louder.

In another hour, Jimmy said they should stop for the night at a motel near Columbia, South Carolina. He drove through two unsatisfactory motels and stopped at the third, where, inside the attached restaurant/lounge Jimmy came up with the idea that Hank should help him meet women. He shared his plan while Hank finished a cheeseburger, fries and Coke and Jimmy finished a steak with whiskey. Jimmy pointed to a woman sitting alone at the bar and told Hank to approach her and say, "Would you like to meet my daddy?"

Hank was shy and didn't want to.

"Just go up to her and ask the question," Jimmy said. "She'll either say yes or no. If she says no, say, thank you anyway. If she says yes, lead her back over here."

Hank didn't want to, but Jimmy wanted him to and Hank wanted to please him, so he did. He rehearsed. "Do you want to meet my father?"

"No. Would you like to meet my daddy?"

"Would you like to meet my daddy?"

"Just like that," Jimmy said. "Hurry, before she leaves."

She was sitting on a high barstool, and Hank's head came to just above her hip, which is what Hank tapped to get her attention. She smiled down at him, flapping her arm in front of his face to wave away cigarette smoke.

She said, "Hey sweetie, what's wrong?"

"Would you like to meet my daddy?"

She stared at Hank. The corners of her mouth moved up, then down. She looked around the room and back to him. Hank pointed to a booth across the room, where Jimmy was staring down into his drink. All of a sudden he looked pretty sad, too. The woman said what the hell, she was all alone, and she put out her cigarette and followed Hank back to Jimmy.

Jimmy stood when they got to the table, towering over everyone. He politely introduced himself, invited her to sit, then ordered her a new glass of wine. They started talking, explaining how they both came to be here at this spot and time in history. Jimmy lit her cigarette with his flip-top silver lighter, and they turned their heads to blow smoke away from Hank. She explained that she was on her way to Ft. Lauderdale from Memphis, taking a vacation from her husband to meet a boyfriend. Jimmy said he'd drink to that. Then he explained how he'd just picked up Hank in Florida. He always said Florida instead of Georgia, which confused Hank until he figured out that Florida must sound prettier than Georgia.

Hank yawned.

Jimmy said, "Hell-fire, let's have one more round."

A waiter brought wine, whiskey, and Coke. The woman pulled out a picture of her daughter and claimed she was close to Hank's age. She said her daughter would fall in love with Hank in a New York minute if she were there. Hank tried to picture her daughter as a Playboy centerfold, but she had too many freckles. When the woman excused herself to go to the bathroom, Jimmy slid the motel-room key across the table and told Hank to go watch television and then go to sleep.

"I'm going to have one more drink," Jimmy said. "Then I'll be along."

Hank did as he was told. He watched *Charlie's Angels*, beautiful women who worked hard to please their invisible boss, laughing and lounging at the end while they gathered around the intercom his voice came through. He watched a late-night movie about other beautiful women being in love with a rich man on a yacht. He watched until he fell asleep. When he woke, three hours later, Jimmy still wasn't in his bed. Hank went looking for him. He put on his shorts and T-shirt and slipped into the size-sixteen cowboy boots Jimmy had left beside the door. He shuffled across the parking lot to keep the boots from coming off. He went back to the lounge, which had grown more crowded and much louder. "Love to Love You, Baby" was playing loudly. Hank knew the song from the tape recorder Kerry Mendelson carried on the school bus. Strange-colored lights swirled around his eyes. He didn't see his father, but he found the bathroom and stepped up to a urinal. A man in the next stall looked down at him, trying to be friendly.

The man said, "How's it hanging there, good buddy?"

Hank looked down at the stream he was making.

The man said, "Nice boots."

Hank finished quickly and went back out, shuffling between all the bodies, weaving through loud voices and laughter and cigarette smoke, ducking beneath glasses people raised above his head. A couple of red-eyed women patted his cheeks and called him "Sugar," but he kept moving, looking for his father. He circled once more and went outside. He looked in their motel room again. He went to the van. The side door was locked, so he banged his fist against it.

The first thing he saw was the end of the pistol his father was pointing at his face. The second thing he saw was his father's penis, which was also pointing. Jimmy lowered the gun and cursed. This was the gun he kept in the glove compartment, which Hank had discovered several hours earlier, and which Jimmy had ordered Hank never under any circumstances to lay a finger on. Hank had asked if it was loaded, and Jimmy said, "What the hell good is an unloaded gun?"

Then the woman came into view—the same woman Hank had approached in the bar. She was pulling her dress over her head. Then she picked up her underwear and her bra and shoved them into her purse. She gathered her shoes and made her way to the door, holding on to Hank's shoulder as she lowered herself to the ground. Then she zig-zagged away in no particular hurry. Jimmy fell back on his butt and frowned. He held the gun across his crotch, and stared out the open door past Hank into the night at some spot that must have been the saddest thing he'd ever seen.

He said, "Get in here and close the door."

Hank crawled in, closed the door, and sat next to him.

Jimmy patted his leg. He sighed. He said, "Did I scare you?"

Hank nodded.

"I'm sorry," Jimmy said. "That won't ever happen again."

Hank thought about the sad spot his father had been staring at and tried to find it, even though the door was closed.

"You like those boots?" Jimmy said.

"Yes."

"We'll try to find you some that fit."

Jimmy got dressed, and they went back to their motel room, where Jimmy fell asleep quickly and started snoring. Hank listened to the rhythm of his father's breathing and tried to match it.

That summer, Hank and his father slept together on the waterbed that took up the entire bedroom of the trailer Jimmy rented. Above the waterbed he'd hung a vinyl painting of a naked woman lying on a bearskin rug. They slept late and stayed up late. They ate their meals in diners, where Jimmy flirted with waitresses who knew his name. Every time a waitress told Hank that he looked just like his father, Jimmy slapped his shoulder, said "Son, *thank* the lady."

Very soon, Hank learned poker. He snapped the face-up cards while dealing seven card stud to his father and to his father's friends, most of whom made up the sales team Jimmy supervised at the cemetery owned by his first cousin, Curtis, who wanted Hank to call him Uncle.

On their first night of playing poker, Hank begged Jimmy for a sip of beer, and Jimmy said no, but Uncle Curtis said, "Give him one."

Jimmy said, "His mother would cut my dick off."

Uncle Curtis said, "One sip will cure him of wanting another one."

Jimmy handed Hank his open beer. He held it with both hands, while the men looked on. He sipped from it. Even the smell was bad, and when he got past the smell, the taste made him want to gag, but he fought it back and smiled, then took another sip.

"Now look what you've done," Jimmy told Uncle Curtis.

"He's not *my* son," Uncle Curtis said, and all the men laughed and the game resumed and when Hank finished that beer he asked for another one, but no one laughed and Jimmy told him to go to bed.

At the end of the second week, Jimmy dropped off Hank and his toothbrush at Uncle Curtis' house so he could go on a date with a woman who would become his fourth wife, a divorced accountant he said he'd been dating a few months, which confused Hank, given the motel incident and the fact that his third wife had left only a month or so before. When Hank asked his father why he'd never mentioned her, he said he was in the habit of keeping his cards close to his vest. Hank knew what he meant. He'd started holding his cards that way too.

Jimmy told Hank he'd be back for him the next morning.

Uncle Curtis had been Jimmy's best man when Jimmy and Hank's mother got married, a fact he explained now at the kitchen table while Hank ate a steak and drank a Coke and Uncle Curtis sipped whiskey.

Uncle Curtis said, "Your mother's a very special lady—beautiful. Talented. Smart. I loved her before your father did. I loved her while they were married. Truth be told, I'm still in love with her."

Hank stopped eating. He wanted to call his mother. He wanted her to come pick him up so he could go home to her and Henry. Uncle Curtis sipped more whiskey. His eyes were nearly closed.

"One of these days," he said, "we'll talk again."

Hank said, "Could I be excused?"

"You can finish that expensive steak."

Hank forced down the rest of his steak and went to bed, feeling dizzy and homesick. He was tired of Uncle Curtis and Jimmy's loud friends, he was tired of Jimmy's smelly trailer, he was tired of eating every meal at a diner, he was tired of being the punchline to his father's jokes with waitresses.

Sometime in the night, Hank got up for some water. He wandered toward a dim light coming from the kitchen and saw Uncle curtis, wearing only boxer shorts, talking on the phone while sitting on the edge of a kitchen chair that faced the cabinet. His chin was level with the counter, but he seemed comfortable enough. His left hand held a whiskey glass and a cigarette. Through the hole in his boxer shorts, his erect penis was protruding. But he wasn't touching it. Hank didn't understand. He imagined a penis in that condition would probably itch very badly, but Uncle Curtis seemed comfortable not touching it. He whispered something in his deep voice that he followed with a laugh.

He said, "I still have a certain amount of expertise in that particular area, my dear."

Hank went back to bed.

The next night, Hank called his mother. He wanted to tell her to come get him. It was Sunday, and he and Jimmy had just returned from a diner, where his father had asked another waitress to marry him. Jimmy said he'd leave him alone so he could talk in private.

Hank's mother said, "Is everything okay?"

"Yes."

"Don't lie if it's not, Hank—you can tell me. Is everything okay?"

Hank said, "What's Dad doing?"

She paused too long, and it made Hank suspicious. It made him wonder whether the next thing she said would be true.

"He's outside."

"Can I talk to him?"

"He's cutting the grass. Are you having a good time?"

It was dark. Hank didn't believe Henry was cutting the grass

"Everything's going to be just fine," she said.

She sounded like she'd been crying, or was about to.

Don't worry about a thing," she said.

"Tell Dad I said hello."

Jimmy entered the room just then, which made Hank feel weirdly disloyal for calling his stepfather *Dad*. Jimmy sank into a chair and lowered his eyes like he'd just gotten bad news.

He said, "I want you to remember something."

Hank stared through the window toward some dark spot of the future.

"I want you to remember that no one will ever love you as much as your mother loves you. That's something I didn't realize until it was too late with my own mother, and I feel guilty about it every day. So you should try to make it as easy on her as you can, okay?"

Hank wondered if Henry would be there when he got back. He remembered Henry waving in the driveway and suddenly doubted it.

"Son?" Jimmy said. "You hear what I said?"

Hank heard his father's voice, but it seemed, already, to be coming from some great distance. He swore to himself just then that he would never, under any circumstances, get so close to a girl that it would require marriage. He thought it would be a great idea, in fact, never again to get too close to a girl. The girl he would start not getting close to the soonest would be Kerry Mendelson, whether she'd developed breasts or not.

He thought of Sister Fermina. He imagined the three-minute walk to her office as a private march no one else could know about. He imagined sitting beneath her yellow bulb, his back stiff with proper posture. He looked forward to her familiar odors. He would see her at nine a.m. on the first day of school, and at nine a.m. every day of his fourth-grade school year, and her heavy and scaly hand would press itself on top of his as they made their way through every letter of the alphabet, printed and cursive, first lower case, then capitals.

Chuck Langford Jr., Depressed Auctioneer, Takes Action

C huck Langford Jr., 61, recovered his voice after three days, but he didn't feel like telling anyone, not even his fifth wife, Dr. Lucy Steele, Ph.D., whom he was fairly certain he still loved after seven years. He was more certain of his love for her than for anyone else he'd ever thought he'd loved, though he had no idea what he'd say if someone stuck a microphone under his nose and pressed him to prove it. Just now, as she entered the kitchen on her way to work, he was leaning against the sink, finishing his bowl of Crispix, still in his pajamas, dreaming out the window toward that place she liked to call his "la-la land." He thought she looked nice. He thought: wouldn't it make her happy for him to say so? He thought so. But wouldn't saying so reveal his recovered voice and require further talk, which he was not, just now, up to performing? Yes. Yes, it would.

He worried that she was onto him. If she *was* onto him, he worried that she might mistake his silence as a statement directed at her, which was not what he intended, entirely. Whether *she* still loved *him* after seven years, he could not, with confidence, say. He certainly didn't want to ask. He felt fairly sure that if a relationship reached a point where each party verbalized simultaneous doubts then it was probably *dead in the water*, to use a phrase his father used fifty years ago just before he blasted a hole in the kitchen ceiling with the shotgun he kept on the table beside his bottle of Early Times. His father had warned that he'd shoot as soon as another person made another sound, then Chuck's beloved beagle, Clarence, yelped, and that was all it took for his dad to shoot his own ceiling. Which is when Chuck's wrist got snatched by his mother, who pulled him out of that house (*without Clarence!*) and into her rusted Plymouth and down that North Carolina mountain road forever, leaving Chuck Sr. at the table with white ceiling-matter in his hair, bills from his auto rust-proofing business (*dead in the water*) stacked on the table, a scene Chuck was sorry he remembered so vividly after so long a time, though he could not remember now having shared this memory with anyone, not even Dr. Lucy, from whom he felt no need to hide anything, except for his recovered voice, temporarily.

Now, Dr. Lucy said, "I get to spend all morning dreading my afternoon meeting with the troglodytes, which amounts to another waste of another day in a life wasted on assholes. How is it that so many pre-verbal infantile men have remained in charge of our inept institutions for so long? Can *you* answer that? If things go badly, I'm prepared to tell them to shove my job straight up their asses and walk out. How would you feel about that, darling?"

Chuck wiped milk off his bottom lip. He nodded to show his support for taking whatever action she felt appropriate. He trusted her to make good choices. She had integrity, something he loved about her. *Integrity* and *courage*—those were words he'd think to use once the microphone moved away.

"I'm very tired," she said. "I'm tired of meeting with Deans and Presidents who interrupt me so they can bicker like three-year-olds.

I'm also tired—I have to tell you—I'm tired of talking to myself around here, which wasn't much different before you lost your voice, if you must know. It just seems more obvious now because you're not talking to yourself anymore either. Something has to change, dear. Something has to change very soon, indeed."

Chuck offered an expression that he hoped conveyed his understanding that something needed to change. She was skilled at reading non-verbals like this because she chaired the Speech and Communications Department at the state college. For five years, she'd talked of quitting so she would never endure another situation like the one she faced today, which Chuck had heard all about last night: her appeal of the firing of her best instructor, Doris Crane, a sixty-year-old adjunct who allegedly insulted a baseball player who fell asleep during her lecture on the art of listening. The baseball player's father, a donor, called the President to complain that his son had suffered emotional distress.

Chuck decided that when Lucy returned this afternoon, he would greet her at the door and start singing "Hell-o, Darling! Well, hell-o. . . ." They'd celebrate his recovered voice over a special dinner he planned to cook. He'd listen while she talked about her day, which was destined to go badly, as most days did these days. He'd recommend resigning immediately so they could finally take their (*her*) nest egg to Costa Rica, where they (she) had long talked of moving in order to kill off the death-inducing day-to-day routine of the same dull place and be dropped into a beautiful new spot, which would be like being born again. "Let's go!" he planned to say tonight. "I'm ready for a change." And he would pound his fist on the table to demonstrate his eagerness.

She leaned against the doorframe and squinted. She said, "You look like you're in pain."

Chuck lifted his chin, pointed to his throat.

She walked downstairs and slammed the door with enough force to shake the walls.

"Right," Chuck announced to the kitchen. "It is time for a change." He put his cereal bowl in the sink, ran no water into it, and looked out the window at a bright cardinal. He had decided, while Lucy was talking, effective immediately, that he would retire from auctioneering. He owed his lost voice—and his current mood—to last week's auction, when he'd stood all day in the August sun, selling another tobacco farm, the scorched land, the broken equipment, the run-down house and all of its worn furniture, including the four chairs he sold right out from under the family who filled them in the puny shade of a dead pecan tree. By dusk, after selling a set of six handmade brooms for $1, his voice was shot. Three days later, when he tested his voice by saying *good morning* to the empty bedroom, he was sorry to hear himself. He had found that not hearing his own voice had been quite soothing. Silent monks were smart: silence was no sacrifice; it was a blessing. Words were like pennies: there were too many in circulation and they had lost their value. People repeated the same words too often for the same purposes: to share bad news, or to complain or to express anxiety or to manipulate. What was the word for using too many words? He knew, once. It was an ugly-sounding word, he remembered that much. Too many words had prolonged his four previous marriages. His own father taught Chuck that unsolicited noise could lead to a broken jaw, which was the injury his father administered a year before he shot his own ceiling, when Chuck passed gas (with excessive sound-effects) after being told to be absolutely still and silent. Words had done his mother no good either, especially in the final year of her life while she suffered from stroke complications, mumbling to tell Chuck something he never understood. Mostly, too many words came spewing too fast from too many people who had too many strong opinions to share, was Chuck's opinion. Educators were the worse. He'd heard them at too many parties, each person waiting for the end of another person's monologue so they could launch their own monologue on some unrelated subject that would show off a very different expertise. Prolix. That was the word that meant using too many words. And while people described him, generally, as "quiet," no one ever accused any of his wife's colleagues as being excessively, endlessly, and painfully "verbose," which was another word he himself would never use.

Something was wrong with him. He wanted to talk to Dr. Lucy about it. He wanted to confess that he'd fallen into the habit of thinking too much about the shape of his shrinking life, such a common practice among people his age that this thought depressed him too. He'd wasted thirty years helping the wrong people (banks/developers) do the wrong things. And zero money at his age = failure! Dr. Lucy had the house, the IRA, the supplemental savings, the investments. He owned an old Studebaker truck that needed a new generator, a new muffler, and new tires.

As a father, he was a failure too. But he planned to change that. He hadn't talked to his unemployed and recently divorced son in a month or more, though he lived just thirty miles away. Shouldn't he call him right this second, just to ask how he was coping? And to ask about his son's one-year-old daughter? Chuck hated to think of her growing up in this sorry world. Would some lunatic shoot her on a playground or in a movie theatre or in a classroom? Would she run out of water or food? Would she ever escape her loud city and enjoy the vanishing countryside? How long would he know her anyway, given the spot on his lung which his doctor, one month ago, wanted another doctor to look at— likely a product of his three-packs-a-day-for-forty-years habit, though he'd stopped five years ago (ample evidence that he *could* make a change, thank you!), spurred by Lucy's ultimatum that he quit or get divorced. He hadn't told her about the spot. But he would tonight, after dessert. Then he'd apologize for his lifeless libido, a condition that deepened his constant desire to drink. Every morning, his first thought was this: if I spend another full day thinking about not drinking, I'll shoot myself in the ear. He'd been sober one year (still *more* evidence that he could change), following a disastrous night that prompted another of Lucy's ultimatums. His sobriety had only given him enough clarity to realize that he would likely die before he could create some meaningful and lasting good for someone he cared about, like his son, or his granddaughter, or Dr. Lucy, which made sobriety seem useless.

"It is time," he announced again to the kitchen, "to snap out of it."

He marched downstairs to the living room. He bent to his knees, and then lay on the floor, prepared to do ten pushups. His eyes went to his bookcase, where he saw his favorite film, Chaplin's *City Lights* (1931).

At six o'clock, Dr. Lucy dropped an eraser board on his stomach. He was anchored in his recliner, still in his pajamas, the big toes of his splayed bare feet pointed east and west. His toenails needed trimming.

"Now," she said. "You can express yourself. I took it from the college today after I resigned. If you feel so moved, you could write me a note supporting my bold action and declaring your love for me. Or you could write me a poem, ha-ha."

When she smiled, Chuck saw that she'd been crying. She'd been at the college twenty-five years, and she liked her job, mostly, and he knew that her quitting had been a courageous gesture performed largely on behalf of Doris Crane.

The room was all wrong to receive her. He had planned to take a shower and shave and open the curtains and be ready at the door to sing out to her. What she saw now, he knew, did not look good. It looked like he hadn't moved all day, which was very close to the truth. Just before she barged in, he'd been following Harold Lloyd—a small-town boy trying to make it in the Big Apple— stumble up a skyscraper toward the clock-hanging climax in *Safety*

Last (1923). He'd seen Harold survive before, but he still worried about him. The beauty of such films did not rely on resolution; they relied on the palpable emotion of single moments inside key scenes, when actors like Harold Lloyd jolted Chuck's heart with reminders of what it felt like to be alive.

Lucy pushed a magic marker into Chuck's palm and closed his fingers around it. She folded a small towel across the arm of his chair. She said, "Here's your eraser."

Harold Lloyd felt most alive when he was close to death, and Chuck felt alive empathizing with the clarity of that feeling. He'd been close to death a couple times himself, but not lately, which meant he hadn't felt too alive at all, something he felt like apologizing for, especially to Dr. Lucy, who had little reason to have enjoyed his lifeless company of late. Just now, he saw her looking down at him as if he were a sick infant. He looked at Harold Lloyd dangle from the big arm of his clock, now pointed at 3, handy for hanging on.

Chuck lifted his hand to Lucy's hand and squeezed it. He wanted to say, "I'm proud of you." He peeked at Harold, still hanging on, then uncapped his magic marker, held the cap in his lips, and drew a smiley face on his new eraser board. He held the board beneath his unshaven chin and smiled above the smiley face, hoping it would make Lucy smile. The long hand of Harold Lloyd's clock started slipping toward six, with Harold still attached. Lucy smiled. She smoothed her hand across Chuck's hair. He wanted to say, *Thank you for being patient while I recuperate from this silly sadness.* He wanted to say, *Hang in there.*

Dr. Lucy said, "Let's celebrate. Light the grill!"

Chuck winced as if a needle had poked his brain.

Lucy pulled back her hand. She had called at noon and talked into the machine, asking Chuck to pick up please if he was there, so he did, saying nothing. She'd said, "How about grilling ribeyes for dinner? Sigh once for yes and twice for no." He'd sighed. She'd said, "Go now and take them from the freezer so you won't forget. Do you love me?" He sighed. He hung up and fell in love with Lillian Gish, again, in *The Wind* (1928), and after that he fell in love with William S. Hart in *Hell's Hinges* (1916), and after that he fell in love with his acrobatic hero Buster Keaton in *The General* (1926), and after that he fell in love with Max Linder (who killed himself in 1941) in *Seven Years Bad Luck* (1921). He drifted through the afternoon this way, forgetting time, until Harold Lloyd hung from his clock and kicked his legs while Dr. Lucy stared down at Chuck, her face dissolving into something too sad for words.

Chuck channeled Chaplin's heartbroken face at the end of *City Lights*, when his lovely flowergirl's restored vision condemns him as a tramp.

Dr. Lucy's eyes held seven years' worth of speeches that could catalogue moments like this. If she were making a speech to a room of young women contemplating marriage, Chuck thought she would do well to show a slide of him as he looked now. The women would laugh and clap and give knowing nods while Dr. Lucy smiled behind her podium and moved to her next slide, a blown-up picture of a sewn-up mouth. These slides made Chuck want to change the way she was looking at him. He watched Harold Lloyd kick from his clock while looking at the concrete far below. He wiped the towel across his smiley face. He wrote, "I'm sorry."

Lucy lifted her heels and frowned, a position Chuck imagined she held in front of her students when their prolonged silences unsettled her.

He drew a vertical line over the period, creating an exclamation mark.

She said, "Do you need to go to the emergency room?"

He underlined 'sorry' in "I'm <u>sorry!</u>"

"Do you need a psychiatrist?"

He raised his chin and touched his adam's apple.

Dr. Lucy walked upstairs, punishing each step in a slow and tired climb.

Harold hung from his clock. He kicked his legs. When he looked down, Chuck's heart grew large with fear. Harold held his heroic poise long enough to survive in a decisive split-second, then he felt more alive than ever, having awakened to a bright new world, which made Chuck feel alive-enough to lower the foot rest on his recliner and start upstairs to whisper his devotion to his wife and fix her something to eat, or go get her favorite dish and bring it back, or take her out to her restaurant of choice, though he'd have to shower first and find clean clothes.

A half-hour later, the phone rang. Chuck held his breath, dreading footsteps in his direction which might require an answer to an auction-related question that would deepen his desire for silence. But there were no footsteps, and he felt relieved.

Ten minutes later, someone knocked on the door. It was Sam, Chuck's best friend, along with Sam's third wife, Linda. Sam and Chuck had been drinking buddies for forty years, but last October, they'd agreed to get sober. They agreed to this following a night when the new owner of their favorite bar engaged them in a gun-control debate. The argument escalated to shouts and curses that led to the new bar-owner's request that both men leave and never darken his door again, the same door they'd been entering for thirty years, whose original owner, Luke Jarvis, they had carried, with help from four other drunk pallbearers, to his grave. Hot with rage at the new bar-owner's nerve, Chuck went to his truck and removed from his glove compartment the handgun he kept there for emergency purposes and returned to the bar to show the new bar-owner that he did in fact carry his very own revolver despite being opposed to the sale and distribution of fully automatic assault weapons, and to prove that the gun was real, Chuck fired a single shot into the ceiling.

Point made, he left peacefully, apologizing to the bar patrons lying on the floor. He returned to his running truck, where Sam was waiting, and in the second part of his three-point turn, backed through the front window of Braun's jewelry store. He was charged with a DWI, aggravated assault and possession of an unregistered firearm. When Linda and Lucy bailed them out, Dr. Lucy, speaking for Linda, told them if they wanted to avoid being divorced and homeless (again), they'd stop drinking immediately and forever.

After their first AA meeting, they went to a bar to discuss what to do in place of meetings. They decided to meet every afternoon at Dale's Diner, the place they'd been visiting since they were sixteen, when it was Dale's Drive-In. They met at 4:30, so they'd be in the diner at 5, the official start of the drinking day. After an hour of coffee, they promised each other they'd go home and kiss their wives with coffee-breath. They'd express gratitude for the homes they shared with their grateful wives. Gratitude was important, they'd learned in their only AA meeting. And it worked. It worked if you worked it. It had been working for the past ten months, including holidays. They said, "One mother-fucking day at a goddamned time, sweet Jesus."

For the last three days, Chuck had listened to Sam, who talked enough for both of them. Today, when Sam called at 4:35 and spoke into the machine, wondering just where the hell Chuck was ("you better not be bellied up to any watering hole without me next to you") Chuck picked up the phone and whispered the truth, that he didn't trust himself to leave the house. Sam said he understood. He said he'd see him tomorrow.

But here he was, blasting through the door in his regular out-fit—red sneakers without socks, baggy shorts to the knees and a white T-shirt. Lucy took Linda upstairs with the bottle of wine Linda brought along, and Sam went to the living room, stood beside Chuck's chair.

Sam said, "I was worried about you." He looked at Fatty Arbuckle carrying a bucket, and shook his head. He turned off the movie and changed the channel to a boxing match. Then he pointed to Chuck's *I'm sorry!* sign and laughed so hard he started coughing. He pulled the eraser board from Chuck's lap and placed it across his chest.

He said, "What we need is to get you some string so you can hang it around your neck. Then you can point to it every time she comes into a room or you go into a room. Hell, what we *ought* to do is make up about a hundred signs just like this, add some string and sell the sons of bitches for ten bucks a-pop to every hen-pecked sorry bastard in the county."

Chuck heard the women laughing loudly upstairs, no doubt sharing stories about the sorry state of men, which Chuck was happy to hear, sincerely, knowing Lucy hadn't laughed much lately, even though he suspected the loudest laughter came at his expense.

He pointed a finger to the ceiling. He said, "She doesn't know I got my voice back."

"Yes, she does. I told her on the phone what you told me, that you were feeling down and didn't trust yourself to leave the house. You should have told me if you wanted that to be a secret. Sometimes you don't communicate too well, Chuck, I'll be honest with you."

Chuck leaned his cheek against his left fist. Sam placed Chuck's *I'm sorry* sign back onto his lap. He said, "You'll need this." And he laughed again, too loudly.

Chuck had planned to announce his recovered voice in bed, before they went to sleep. He had planned to wake up next to her and say, "Good Morning!" He had imagined that she'd be pleased to hear his voice, which meant the rest of the morning, maybe the entire day (the rest of their lives?) would be full of happy sounds.

Sam provided expert commentary over the voices of the boxing experts. He said, "That guy in the red needs to change tactics.

He can't stand toe to toe with that big man. He's got to jab and dance, jab and dance, jab and dance." At the end of that fight, the boxers hugged. Sam said, "I never have understood how you could hug somebody who was trying to kill you. Do you understand that? I've never understood that. Like they're saying, hey, sorry about all that brain injury, you know I love you, right?"

Three fights later, Linda came downstairs with Dr. Lucy to say it was time to go. Sam hugged Dr. Lucy and Chuck hugged Linda. Chuck closed the door, happy to be alone with Lucy in their quiet home. He put a hand on her shoulder, bent to kiss her. She ducked, staggered, righted herself against the closed door, and pressed her index finger against his lips.

She said, "Chuck? We need to talk."

He stuck his hands in his armpits, raised his chin, and looked into her eyes.

He moved into Sam's mildewed basement, slept on a thrift-store mattress. He came and went as quietly as he could, but Linda had sided with Lucy and she didn't like the idea of sheltering him. Above him, the arguments between Sam and Linda grew louder, and he knew he was the cause. For money, he auctioned off a foreclosed home, and he filled in once for the old man who normally worked the cattle auction, but he'd had to replace his truck's generator, then its radiator, which left scarce money for gas and food. He went to Dale's Diner for breakfast, returned for lunch, then went back at 4:30 for coffee with Sam, which he followed with dinner after Sam went home to Linda. Dale had agreed to give him a line of credit Chuck swore he'd pay at the end of the month.

One week later, a Friday at 4:30, Chuck walked in and waved at Dale, who stood in his white uniform in the kitchen, as he had for fifty years, then he greeted an elderly couple and claimed his regular table at the window, which held a dust-covered "For Sale" sign. Edna, the eighty-year-old hostess, cashier, waitress, and wife of Dale, sat at the next table, reading Sam's weekly newspaper.

Chuck said, "Edna? You know a place in town where I can get a cup of coffee?"

She licked her finger and turned a page. She said, "If you don't know by now, they ain't much hope for you."

He went behind the counter, lifted a cup from a tray of cups, poured his own coffee, and returned to his table.

He said, "Don't you ever get sick of this place?"

"I've been sick of it since I was taking your order on roller-skates. You tipped me then about what you tip me now, matter-a-fact."

"Let's make a change," Chuck said. "You want to run off together?"

She licked her finger and turned another page. She said, "Shit. You can't make a change." Then she said, "Aw, hell, Roger Church died. Lung cancer, about your age."

In the voice of a child, Chuck said, "I can too make a change." He looked out at the chicken plant across the street where five hundred workers had recently been laid off and conceived a brand new plan.

He said, "Edna, does that payphone on the back wall work? The one next to the jukebox that doesn't work?"

"It works when you put a quarter in it."

"Can I borrow a quarter?"

She shook her head and looked up at the door, which Sam was just now bursting through, box beneath one arm. He went straight for the coffee, greeted the old-timer regulars, gave a shout to Dale, and a "Hello, pretty lady" to Edna, and dropped his box on Chuck's table. He sipped his coffee and opened the box, pulled out a white T-shirt and held it beneath his chin. Printed boldly across the shirt in all-caps were the words I'M SORRY. He removed another shirt and tossed it to Chuck. He said, "Look here, Edna."

Edna looked. She said, "Why would you advertise the obvious?"

Sam said, "Edna, we'd like to make amends to you for all the many years of mistreatment you have endured at the expense of men like me and Chuck, especially Chuck. I hope you'll find it in your big heart to forgive us." Sam looked more sincere and humble than Chuck had ever seen him.

Edna said, "Y'all plan on eating, or you just taking up a table?"

Sam said, "I'm going to my Rotary meeting, where I plan to preach the gospel of gratitude, forgiveness, and free-enterprise, then I'm going to sell this box of T-shirts, which is going to put me late getting home, but I'll wear one in the door, see if Linda notices."

"Give me a quarter," Chuck said.

Sam pulled a quarter from his pocket and put it on the table. Chuck flung his T-shirt over his shoulder, and took the quarter to the payphone. He pulled a piece of paper from his wallet and dialed the number written on it. A thin voice answered on the first ring. The *hello?* sounded like a pitiful question ready to receive bad news.

"Charlie?" Chuck said. "This is your father. I'm coming to pick you up so you can help me do this thing I want to do." In the background, a loud television played.

Charlie paused. He said, "Now?"

"Now."

"You remember where I live?"

"Of course I do."

"And your truck's going to make it up the mountain?"

"I'll see you in a half-hour."

Chuck went back to his table, reached into Sam's box and pulled out two more shirts. He said, "Put these on my tab."

Sam said, "Tell Edna you're sorry for not leaving a tip."

"I love you, Edna," Chuck said. He had made a serious effort to sound sincere, but he wasn't sure it came across. He said, "Edna, I'm being sincere."

"Fuck off," she answered.

"That's my girl," Sam said.

He started the steep climb up the mountain from Wilkes County to Boone, four and a half cylinders clacking and wheezing, sunburned arm propped out of his window, tractor-trailers blaring past him on the left. On the way, he tried to think of what he wanted to tell his son. Charlie had graduated last year (a *Math* major?), but he hadn't found a job and he'd continued drinking, then the baby came too soon, as they do, so his wife took the child to Tennessee to live with her parents, claiming it was temporary. Chuck wanted to cheer up his son. He wanted to tell him that resilience was the most valuable asset one could own. Then he'd spread his arms and say "Just look at me." And they might laugh, and the mood would turn, and Chuck would start to feel—for the first time in a long time—useful.

An hour later, he knocked on doors in his son's apartment complex. Three college students shrugged and apologized. The fifth door he came to had a piece of paper stuck to it—a notice from the electric company that power would be disconnected in three days unless a payment was rendered. Chuck knocked. A soft voice said, "Come in?" Chuck stepped into a living room that held only a recliner and a television. Gunfire came from men on galloping horses. Charlie occupied the recliner, wearing only underwear, bare feet pointed east and west. Beside his recliner, a pizza box held spent cigarettes and crushed beer cans.

"Shit," Chuck said. "She took everything?"

"Not *every*thing." Charlie pointed toward the television, which sat on the floor.

"How can you buy cigarettes, beer, pizza, and cable when you can't pay the light bill?"

"What?"

Chuck pulled the remote from his son's hand and turned off the television. He pointed toward a fist-sized hole in the white plastered-wall. "What happened here?"

"A fist," Charlie said.

"Spread some flat newspaper in there and cover it with spackling, you might get your security deposit back." He tossed a shirt into his son's lap. "Put this on and find some pants."

"Where we going?"

"I'll tell you when we get there." Chuck regretted saying this. It reminded him of what his own father had said the few times he took him somewhere, which usually ended up being a bar, where he'd say, "Wait in the car while I go see somebody about some money."

Charlie unfolded the shirt and looked at it. He said, "You want me to wear this?"

"I have one too." Chuck pulled off the old T-shirt he was wearing, then pulled on his 'I'm Sorry!' shirt. It was too small. He said, "What size do you have?"

Charlie looked at the tag. "Small," he said. "Why are we sorry?"

Chuck scratched his cheek. He puckered his lips. He said, "I'll tell you on the way."

But the loud truck made talking difficult—they kept the windows down because the air conditioner didn't work, and the old engine and the bad muffler sounded like a train. The trip wouldn't be long enough to cover as much history as Chuck needed to cover, and still, he didn't know where to start. Charlie wasn't eager to talk anyway. He lit his second cigarette and stared at his phone.

He drove beyond Boone into Vilas and pointed down Linville Creek Rd. He said he had a great friend from many years ago who lived down there that he should pay a visit to. Charlie stared at his phone. In ten more miles, Chuck turned up a narrow road that wound up and around a series of tight curves that continued uphill past three cows, a donkey, a llama, an old tractor with a metal seat parked outside a collapsed barn. The asphalt turned to gravel and the gravel turned to dirt, and the road narrowed and kept going up and around and up and around until the road stopped in front of a tin-roofed shack rusted so deeply it looked burnt. The house sloped toward the right front corner, as if the foundation there had crumbled. Occupying the center of the sagging porch was a long-bearded man in a wheelchair who was pointing a shotgun toward Chuck's advancing head.

"What the fuck?" Charlie said. "Stop."

Chuck kept going. He went twenty more yards, close enough to look down the barrel into the old man's squinted eye.

Charlie raised both hands inside the cab. He yelled, "Don't shoot." To his father, he whispered, "Back up. Back up slowly."

"He won't shoot," Chuck said. "He thinks we're the IRS or the FBI or lost revenuers."

The gun sounded like a bazooka. Gravel and dirt kicked up in front of the truck and splattered the grill.

Charlie hit the floorboard. He said, "Haul ass, man. Hit it. *Retreat!*"

"Ha." Chuck pushed his head out of his window. He said, "My name's Chuck Langford."

The old man kept his gun raised. He said, "Who wants to know?"

Chuck opened his door and stepped out. He held the shirt by his side and stood still, feeling brave and curious and *alive*.

"You're crazy," Charlie said. "*I'm* not getting out."

"He won't shoot again." Toward the old man, he shouted, "I'm Chuck Langford *Junior*. That makes me your son."

The second shot blew a patch of grass and dirt onto the tops of Chuck's shoes.

"Holy fucking shit," Charlie said. "Are you hit?"

"Very nice," Chuck said. He took two steps forward. He said, "I'm your *son*, Chuck T. Langford *Jr*. This is your grandson." He pointed his thumb behind him, then turned to see an empty cab.

Chuck said, "Charlie, sit up so your grandfather can see you."

"Fuck that," Charlie said.

Chuck Sr. said, "You got a cigarette? I'll trade you a beer for a cigarette."

"I don't smoke," Chuck said. "I quit. You should too."

"*I've* got a cigarette!" Charlie raised a cigarette out his window and held it high.

Chuck Sr. lowered his gun. He said, "Y'all come on ahead."

Chuck and Charlie walked uphill toward the porch. The woods on three sides made the same nest of the house that Chuck remembered, but the woods seemed thinner now, and dry. Just in front of the woods, his father's 1960 Studebaker truck was melting into the earth. Weeds grew through the hoodless engine block and through the space where the windshield had been. The cab's roof was rusted the color of red clay. Three chickens pecked around a propane tank. Torn sheets of plastic hung from two front windows.

When Chuck and Charlie got to the porch, they each propped a foot on the wheelchair ramp, two pieces of warped plywood supported by cinderblocks, speckled with chicken shit. His father's right leg was gone. Above the untrimmed beard that grew high on his cheeks, his dim blue eyes were filmy, probably cataracts. His father reached for the cigarette Charlie extended toward him, put it in his mouth and let Charlie light it for him. He inhaled, blew smoke back out, picked at something on his tongue.

"Goddamn menthol," he said. But he raised the cigarette again and squinted at his son. He gave him the kind of look Chuck had seen from too many men in bars who administered the quick-study read of a face's fighting history—the wins and defeats and knockouts and the size of the neck and head which measured the kind of punch a man could take. Chuck lifted his shoulders and straightened his spine and squinted back at his father, but his father had already looked away, toward Charlie, whose small head was hanging by a thin neck, eyes pointed toward the ground, skinny arm propped on skinny thigh, looking like he'd already lost a fight as recently as this morning. He was too thin, maybe 140 pounds.

Chuck Sr. said, "Y'all 'bout got yourselves shot. They's been some crackheads around here stealing anything ain't nailed down. Cocksuckers stole my rooster."

Chuck looked into the open house—there was no door—and saw a knee-deep trail of clothes and shoes, box-lids and newspapers that led to the kitchen where a chainsaw sat on top of the stove next to a jar of pigs' feet. A chicken walked out of the hall and disappeared into the kitchen. All the wallpaper had peeled away, and black mold ran along the baseboards. Even from the porch, Chuck smelled mildew and garbage, strong as a decaying corpse.

Charlie said, "How 'bout that beer, gramps?"

Chuck said, "Last time I saw you, you were shooting guns *inside* the house, came close to killing me then too."

"If I'da meant to kill you, you'd be dead." He brought the cigarette to his lips again, blew smoke. He said, "You come here looking to inherit my fortune? Or you come here to tell me something? Something you need to tell me before I die?"

Charlie said, "I could use that beer. I'll get it if you don't want to get up."

Chuck looked inside again. He'd missed it before because of all the junk on top of it, including the front door, which leaned against it, but there against the near wall in the same spot was the upright piano his mother had taught him to play. The round swivel stool was pushed beneath it, legs wrapped in thick spider webs. She had sworn he had great talent, and she had talked for many years of wishing she could go back and get it, but she'd been too afraid that the man in front of him now would hurt someone.

Chuck Sr. said, "I'm surprised you didn't have to bring your mother with you."

"She died ten years ago. She died a slow and painful death after having a hard life you had a lot to do with."

Chuck Sr. squinted above his son's head back toward the road. He said, "Well."

"Is that beer in the fridge?" Charlie said.

Chuck tossed the shirt onto his father's lap. "I brought this for you. In case you can't stand to say the words and just want to hold it up. That'd be enough for me."

Chuck Sr. held it up and looked it over, front and back. He squinted toward the shirts Charlie and Chuck Jr. wore. He said, "I'm half-blind and can't see to find my glasses. What's it supposed to say?"

"Says I'm sorry,'" Chuck Jr. said.

"What?"

"I'm sorry," he shouted.

Sr. nodded, apparently pleased. He paused. He said, "Now then. Was that so hard?"

Chuck laughed. At first, it was a single "ha," then the laugh caught fire and felt good—it was the first good laugh he'd had in a good long time, and it filled the air and the valley below and echoed all around them—an epic laugh stored fifty years, fueled by all the times he thought he'd seen his father coming or going through town or standing at the rear of one of his auction crowds, though it was always someone else, or no one.

Charlie said, "Who needs a beer?"

Chuck Sr. said, "They ain't no beer, son. I ran out this morning. I lied about that to get this lousy cigarette. You ought not to trust every stranger you meet. Maybe your Daddy never taught you that, but mine did. That's about all he taught me, but it was enough. What you ought to do is run fetch us a carton of cigarettes and a case of beer. You come back first of the month, I'll get the next round. My last wife left me last December. I can't keep a woman. Judging by the hang-dog looks of you, I'm betting you'ns have the same luck."

Chuck and Charlie looked up at the old man who was now scratching his beard and looking above their heads toward the road, squinting. He licked his lips, scratched his beard again, seemed to be thinking something serious. He lifted the T-shirt from his lap, balled it up and threw it back at his son. The shirt hit Chuck in the face and fell down to his stomach where he caught it.

"It don't fit," Chuck Sr. said.

They stared at each other, saying nothing.

Chuck Sr. said, "Y'all want to bring a proper peace offering, bring some cigarettes and beer. Hell-fire, you come back with groceries, I'll invite you inside."

Chuck hung the shirt over the porch railing so the words faced the road. He said, "I've hated you a long time, but it never did me any good. I carried that hatred around like dead weight, turned it in on myself too, which led to too much drinking and lots of mistakes, but I should've blamed myself for all that a long time ago instead of you. I'm sorry I haven't forgiven you sooner. It would've helped me be a better father, which is something else I'm sorry for—being a bad father." He turned to Charlie. He said, "Son, I'm sorry I've been a bad father."

Charlie shrugged. He said, "I haven't been the greatest son in the world."

Chuck Sr. said, "I tell you what. Go get us a carton of smokes and a case of beer, and I'll let you sit around and apologize all day."

Chuck Jr. looked inside again. He wondered how long it would take to clean the floor, patch the walls, replace the rotten boards around the windowsills and on the porch.

He turned to Charlie. He said, "Let's go."

They turned and walked. After ten steps, the shotgun went off behind them. Charlie jumped, then ducked, then turned and raised his arms over his head and walked backwards. Chuck Jr. didn't flinch. He said, "He's not aiming for flesh."

Chuck Sr. said, "I just wanted to see you jump one time. Y'all bring me back a couple boxes of .12 gauge shells too. Those crackheads will be wandering around after dark, looking to take advantage of a blind old cripple who's all alone."

Chuck Jr. didn't answer. He got into his truck and performed a deliberate three-point turn, then slowly moved ahead. Charlie sat beside him, silent, but Chuck could tell already that in the space between them now there lived the beginning of a story they'd share for a long time to come.

Charlie lit a cigarette. He said, "You're telling me I've lived in the same town with my grandfather all this time and never knew it?"

"Looks that way," Chuck said.

Charlie shook his head. "Anything else I can help you with that might get me shot?"

Chuck scratched his cheek. He said, "I'd like to visit your mother."

Charlie laughed at this. He laughed a little too loudly and a little too long.

"No," Charlie said. "That's three hours away, and she's not—"

"I know how far it is."

"She's not exactly—"

"You have anything else to do?" Chuck said. "Any pressing engagements?"

"No, but I'm warning you, she's not—"

"Alright then," Chuck said. "That'll give us time to talk. I'll tell you all about my dad and all the years we spent not talking. I'll tell you what happened the last time I saw him, when he blew a hole in the kitchen ceiling. I'll tell you about the time he broke my jaw. I'll tell you about the time he broke my mother's jaw. I'll tell you—I wonder how he lost that leg. I bet he shot *himself*, don't you? Probably shot himself while he was drunk. I'll tell you about your grandmother too—you knew her a little bit, but there was a lot you didn't know about all the shit she endured for too long.

There's a lot to talk about, but we have a long way to go, so that's good, and I have a big plan I'd like to share with you. You hungry?"

"What?" Charlie said.

Chuck leaned his son's way, spoke more loudly. "We'll go visit your mother, and then in a few days or a week or so, we'll visit your grandfather again. I think there's something he still wants to tell me. We'll give him another chance. I'd kind of like to fix up that house. What would you think of that? We could fix up that house and maybe even move in. You any good with carpentry? I'm not. I never learned anything from him, and you never learned anything from me, but how hard could it be to nail a new tin roof over the old tin roof and replace some rotten boards and scrub down the place? I thought about asking him if we could auction off the house and the land and then all move into town, but he wouldn't want that, and I got to looking around there and thought, why not save the old homeplace and have a peaceful spot to live? We both need somewhere to live, right? We'll save that house. In three more months, I'll be on the government gravy train, so that'll help. We could make it work. You know? Why not? You have any better ideas? It's a good start, which is all anybody can ask for—a good start. I think he was on the verge of an apology. Did you see that? I think he was softening up a bit. With any luck, he'll croak soon and leave me the estate, which I'll leave to you, which you can leave to your daughter. See how that works? That's the way it's *supposed* to work. Once we get it fixed up, we'll go *get* your daughter and bring her here for a visit. She'll like it so much she'll want to stay. I'll help you raise her. I'd be a goddamn good grandpa."

Charlie leaned over, looking toward the gauges. He said, "You got any gas money?"

"No. You?"

"No."

"It doesn't take any gas to get *down* the mountain. But we'd better scare up a little money for later. Let's go down Linville

Creek Rd., see if my old friends are home. Finest people you'll ever want to meet. I can't remember the last time I saw them."

"You remember where they live?"

"Of course I do."

He would recognize the house when he saw it. Then he wondered if he owed them an apology for some bad thing he may have done during his heavy drinking days. Probably. He planned a proactive approach. He'd simply point to his shirt and smile. And they'd laugh and give him a hug and greet his son and usher them inside and offer them a drink, which Chuck would politely decline, citing his sobriety, which they would congratulate him for. They might insist that he and Charlie stay for dinner, an invitation he'd accept with the sincerest gratitude. Otherwise, they'd have to drive all the way back to Dale's Diner, where he'd have to ask Dale if he could charge his food *and* his son's food. And Dale would say okay, but only after he gave Chuck the same look he'd given him last time, which said there shouldn't be too many more charges before a little something was applied to what was owed.

"Yes," Charlie said now. "I'm hungry."

"I know," Chuck said. "We'll fix that."

If he couldn't find their house—which was seeming more a possibility (wasn't it Linville Creek they lived on?)—he'd knock on a stranger's door and someone would kindly point the way. Strangers were generally eager to help. That's the thing he planned to teach his son. Most strangers were nicer than most family members was his experience, so long as you disclosed your honest intentions and didn't ask for too much and didn't overstay your welcome and could share a simple good word about the weather and could look into another person's eyes with the clarity of knowing your first and last words should be an apology. That's all it took to survive like a king in the company of strangers.

Snell's Law

When he wasn't working, my father lived on our roof with his telescope and his booze. There were times, late at night, when I heard him dancing up there. He was a licensed psychopharmacologist, but I never knew what that meant. When I asked him once what it meant, he told me it was a title given one who specialized in psychopharmacology. I didn't know what that meant either, but I was embarrassed to tell him so. He expected me to know these things.

He took me to the roof when I was young. I looked down his pointed arm toward the constellations he pointed at for me, but I never saw the first. Not even the Big Dipper. I saw every star, but I never saw an example of what some of them group to form. He stopped pointing the year I turned seven. After that, I snuck to the roof when he wasn't home. I used his telescope to look through our neighbors' windows at the wives and daughters of my dad's friends.

My mother was a painter, and we were very much alike, except that I couldn't paint. She painted for happiness, but if it worked, she kept it to herself. When I enrolled in the local community college (instead of leaving home for college as she'd wanted), she stopped talking. She wrote a note to us then that said, "I can't speak without crying, so I'm talking only to my paintings for awhile." My father said she'd suffered a breakdown "of an all-too-common-sort." She didn't ask for help, and he didn't offer any. He said she might get better and she might not; we'd have to keep watching. He asked if I had questions. I could not, just then, think of any.

On a Wednesday night in October of that year, Mom was painting when I came home from flunking my weekly test in my astronomy lab. She was working in a frenzy at the kitchen table without much light, spreading dark oil paints on an oval canvas while a Spanish guitar played from the living room. When I said, "Where's Dad?" she pointed her brush at the ceiling.

I found him mumbling to himself while he looked through his telescope toward the moon. He had a glass in one hand and a bucket of ice between his feet with a bottle stuck in it. When I cleared my throat, the noise startled him so severely that he almost fell head-first to our driveway. I imagined Mom asking me to shovel his brains into a bag. Then I imagined dumping the bag on my bedroom floor so I could study the contents for secrets that could help me.

"What?" he said. "Speak up."

"I'm having trouble in my astronomy class."

"You're having trouble in *all* your classes."

He knew this, I assumed, through conversations he'd had with my instructors. He sipped his drink and stared at me above his glass. He knew them all. I'd known for awhile that they knew I was his son, and I knew he must've been embarrassed at this.

He said, "Tell me. What deficiency in your character do you suppose is most responsible for your sub-mediocre performances?"

I knew the answer to this. I'd given it considerable thought. I'd come to a tentative hypothesis many months before and continued revising it until I reached a level of clarity I could clearly articulate. I wrote my conclusion on a 3x5 index card and memorized it to recite at just this occasion. I paused to find the authoritative tone I'd practiced while facing my bathroom mirror. I looked at the green glob of paint stuck to the toe of my left tennis shoe—a glob Mom dropped from her brush some months ago when I asked for money—so I wouldn't be distracted.

I said, "The primary explanation for my sub-mediocre performance can be attributed to my phenomenal peripheral vision, which prevents me from focusing on one stimulus in multi-stimulied environments in which perfunctory tasks are assigned. The great majority of our required tasks are quite perfunctory in nature. All environments—excepting black holes and sense-deprivation chambers used as punishment or as migraine treatments—contain vast collections of competing stimuli. Therefore, my phenomenal peripheral vision—existing inside a task-centric universe over-crowded with excessive and competing stimuli—prevents me from performing at a level above sub-mediocrity."

But he hadn't heard me. He was looking through his telescope toward the moon. I looked there too. I saw a world of white with puddles of blue. I imagined a crater holding a pillow and a blanket for me there.

He said, "What's the distance from here to there?"

He'd told me this before, many times. I said, "I don't remember."

"Approximately 238,885 miles."

We paused to appreciate the distance to the moon. He dropped two ice cubes into his glass, then emptied his bottle into it.

He said, "Since you were two years old, I've devoted a lot of thought to the way you think. And I'm afraid it's come to this." He jerked his telescope toward me like a machine-gunner in an Army jeep, then jumped behind it, adjusted a knob, curved his mouth into a triangle and stared at the blank face I held three feet away.

"Your nose," he said. "It's a fertile breeding ground for blackheads."

"You told me that yesterday."

"I've designed a device that will solve the problem you describe, a problem which is old news to me. The device is called a *focus-finder*. It comes in the form of a headgear apparatus meant to point your attention toward the most appropriate stimulus in view. A wide cardboard tube—like a larger version of the tube inside a paper towel roll—will encircle your face and extend forward for two feet. This tube encircling your face will remain fastened to your head by a four-inch-wide industrial-strength band of rubber." He lifted his head above his telescope to show me four inches between his thumb and index finger, then ducked again behind his toy.

I was told to wear it to every class. I was told to wear it while reading textbooks. It was a good idea, he added, to wear it while reading menus in expensive restaurants. He came to me then and placed his non-drink-holding hand around my shoulder. He squeezed. He lifted his drink toward the moon. He said, "The Milky Way is waiting for you, son." His voice turned softer than I'd ever heard it. He sniffed so loudly I was sure that he was crying. I looked at the moon and the stars and imagined great things ahead of me. I sniffed too. Then I saw a blinking star moving across the sky that appeared not lower, but in front of all the rest.

I said, "Dad? To what constellation does that blinking star belong?"

He paused. He moved his hand from my shoulder. He said, "That's not a blinking star, son. That's an airplane." He spread a palm across his face. He stared, between his fingers, toward the moon. He moaned. He turned up his drink until it was gone.

I moved to the ladder and descended, ashamed of the question I'd asked, frightened that I would never outgrow the deficiency in my character that produced such thoughts.

The following Wednesday, I walked to my astronomy lab with visions of being successful. I stared at the square-tiled floor of the hall and rehearsed the greeting I'd use to greet my instructor, who was in the habit of greeting students at the door.

"Evening," I said, without breaking stride. I thought: choosing the word "evening," would make him think I was both astute and sensitive for the following reasons: (1) It was evening. (2) By denouncing the universal qualifier of a subjective expression (leaving the "good" off of "evening"), I avoided a non-scientific judgement on the success of his night.

Walking three steps ahead of me was my lab partner, an astute and sensitive young woman that I was determined, by semester's end, to ask for a date that would lead to an engagement that would lead to a happy marriage that would lead to the production of children we'd raise to be happy. I sat on the stool beside her stool at the rectangular wooden table that held a faucet without a sink.

I cleared my throat. I said, "Evening."

She smiled politely and opened a notebook to a page of notes.

The instructor—a bald man with a black beard who spoke with an interesting dialect of origins unknown to me—distributed a test covering material covered in last week's lab. There were windows in the room. Against the windows were reflected the faces of students sitting next to them. An air conditioner clicked on and flipped a switch in my brain that hummed in pitch to the humming air conditioner. On the wall adjacent to the windows, a black and white periodic table hung on a yellow cinderblock wall, a pattern of squares mismatched on a pattern of rectangles, higher on the right side than the left, strips of duct-tape applied to every corner. One fluorescent light behind me and to the right remained burnt out, as it was last week and the week before.

I thought not of answering the questions I could not answer; I thought of the jeopardy I'd placed myself in by failing to focus the week before. It was an open note test. All I had to do was listen last week and take notes so I could copy them onto this week's test. This was legal.

My lab partner took her completed test to our black-bearded bald instructor, who thanked her for doing so.

I read question number one: "What do Theta 1 and Theta 2 have in common?" Below these words was a diagram of a long arrow holding many numbers with decimal points.

I thought: what's a theta? A *Star Wars* character came to mind, but that was all. I wrote, "Theta 1 and Theta 2 are chronological in sequence; Theta 2 comes second to Theta 1."

Our instructor said, "Since we now have all the tests, we can proceed with this evening's exercise."

Question number two said: "In what phase was the moon last night?" I imagined the view from inside the crater that held my pillow and my blanket. I wrote: "From the comfort of a crater, the moon's phase seems irrelevant."

Our instructor started talking of an astronomical law named after a man named Snell. He pointed to some words on the board behind him. His words got caught in his beard. I felt myself drifting. My self said there was little I could do. I stared at my instructor. I thought: I bet I'm impressing my lab partner with what appears to be my intense ability to concentrate. I thought: she's thinking how utterly astute and sensitive a man must be to listen so well to an instructor whose words live inside his beard.

She removed a triangular-shaped glass object from a drawer. She straightened a blank piece of paper on our table, placed a ruler over the center of the page and lifted her pencil. She looked at me. Her irises, behind her glasses, were a watery kind of blue that seemed to be orbiting moon-shaped pupils.

She said, "Do you remember what he said to draw first?"

"Yes. You mean what he said to draw first?"

Her lower lip separated from her upper lip. I stared into her mouth.

She went to the table next to ours and talked to a guy wearing a backwards baseball cap. When she smiled, he showed her his paper. I looked behind me at the homely girl sitting alone whose entire face was so crowded with piles of acne it made me want to close my eyes and offer her a hug for the loneliness I know she suffered. She pushed her paper toward me so I could see the triangle she drew. I drew a triangle too.

She said, "Draw a perpendicular line intersecting the base."

A bright color came to mind. I tried it.

She said, "That's not a perpendicular line."

I began to cry for those who were illiterate and for my own failed future. I looked to the board and saw the dusty path an eraser created. At the top right corner of the chalkboard, these words were printed in tiny script: "Snell's Law: The index of refraction of a transparent medium is equal to the ratio of the speed of light in a vacuum to the speed of light in the medium." I pictured pictures of stars pregnant with disfigured fractions.

The instructor talked to a student excited to debate Snell's Law. My ex-lab partner was wearing her new hero's baseball cap. She pulled the bill of the cap too low and shared a laugh with him.

I folded up the piece of paper with the triangle and the line I drew and took it to my father to show him the mess I'd made. When I reached the roof, he was staring through his telescope into Mrs. Mabry's bedroom window. He held a drink in one hand and his crotch in the other. He made grunting noises. I rattled the ladder to announce my presence, but the noise scared him and he screamed.

"Great Jehovah," he said. "Why do you sneak up on me like that?"

"I'm a failure, Dad."

"Just try to be louder." While he looked at me, he reached behind him to move his telescope from Mrs. Mabry's window toward the moon.

"I mean I've failed another astronomy test."

"I've already heard. Did you wear the focus-finder I left in your bedroom?"

"I forgot it."

"Of course you did. I should have shown you the inspiration for the focus-finder, a miniature model you can apply in any context." He cupped his hands around his eyes like someone staring toward the horizon with a pair of binoculars. His fingers touched in the center of his forehead and his thumbs touched beneath his nose.

"This," he said, "we will call your *plowing-mule-face*. It's what farmers use on their mules when plowing—leather blinders that block the periphery and force the focus to a single row. Imagine yourself as a mule in the middle of a field many acres wide— would you refuse to move if you saw how much more you had to do? I'd say so. Horse trainers also equip their race horses with blinders—or *blinkers*—to prevent distractions from crowds or other horses. They're also sometimes used for high-strung horses or mules to reduce transport-related anxiety. For your purposes, however, I prefer the plowing-mule-face metaphor. Try it."

His entire head was framed by my cupped hands. Three long hairs sprouted from the end of his nose, waving like wind-blown weeds.

"Well?" he said. "Can you see it helping?"

I saw it helping. I saw him so well that it gave me the inspiration to free myself from him. I thought: if I were capable of articulating the chain of images that flashed across my mind just now to reveal my life as an artist, he would be impressed. I saw my first piece: a sculpture of my father's head three times its normal size assembled from glued toothpicks, propped atop the tallest and brittlest tree inside a forest he'd never dare to enter. I saw my second piece: a collage of shredded textbooks meshed with soiled underwear covered with golden stars stolen from kindergarten teachers. I heard an epic poem demanding dictation. I heard a five-movement piece for strings (with soft banjo) in the key of G. I heard the story of this moment. I thought: if he knew I was electing to bypass my attempt to articulate these images in favor of applying my inspiration into immediate practice, he'd be moved to tears.

I turned away. I went to the ladder and descended.

I went to the kitchen so I could tell my mother I was leaving home.

She dropped her brush and cried all over the splotchy oils that covered the canvas that covered the table. She rubbed magenta beneath her eyes. She sobbed for awhile and mumbled some wet words until two of them rose clearly and floated in the space between us.

They sounded like "So proud, so proud," but it took me many years to understand them.

Nothing Ruins a Good Story
Like an Eyewitness

You got it wrong, son. You exaggerated the wrong things and failed to exaggerate the right things. I know you're supposed to know your business, but you wrote your story from a long way off and tried to make it sadder than it was. In your story, I shoot myself. I know you meant well, but you're young and your life has been different than mine, so maybe your imagination isn't mature enough just yet. The other problem is that you don't believe in luck. You don't believe, more specifically, that bad luck plays favorites. But it does, and it has, and that's the story I mean to tell—again.

Three weeks before Christmas (*not* Christmas Eve), I was sitting up late at night holding a handgun. I'd been into a bottle of bourbon, and I was marching along inside a self-loathing campaign to end self-loathing. I was 61, broke and jobless, eyes and feet failing from diabetes, and no family to speak of except for a son who disliked salesmen. The *only* reason I was still alive is that your mother let me live in the backyard studio apartment she'd converted from a shed—"the condo," as she called it. It'd been five years since I pulled into her yard with everything I owned crammed into my car, fresh from leaving my fifth wife. I'd driven eight hours from the Carolina mountains to the south Georgia flatlands, gambling your mother would take pity on me. I was grateful. Even with the slanted ceiling I bumped my head against, even with pecans smacking the tin roof like bombs all through the night. I was grateful to have a single friend who had a spare bed, and I told her so.

But you left out *five years*. It screws up the whole timeline, and your story amounts to one crazy night with no underpinning. You ignored how hard I tried. Every day for five years, my phone machine called a thousand numbers between Savannah and Jacksonville, targeting senior citizens who needed final expense insurance to offset burial costs (I bought some for myself, by the way). Every day, people waited for the end of my one-minute message just so they could record profanities and threats. I was happy to get one lead out of a thousand calls, lucky to sell one a month, and grateful if my commission check arrived a month after that.

I added water to the soup. I survived. Pretty soon, your Mom asked if I ever intended to pay rent. I wanted to, believe me, but every few months, I got further behind and things got so bad that I asked her for small loans—fifty dollars here and there for groceries. I felt guilty every time I asked, and the guilt never went away. On that night in early December, I reached a new low. I called to see if *you* could spare a loan.

"No problem," you said.

I knew I'd interrupted something. I heard music and voices and silverware clinking on plates, and then I felt worse. Here you were, about to bring your future ex-spouse home to meet your parents, and here was your father, calling up to advertise his problems.

I said, "I'm embarrassed to have to ask."

"No problem," you said again.

"Yes it is," I said. "I was married to a teacher once; I know what you make. The father is supposed to help the child," I said. "Not the other way around."

"I understand," you said.

"No you don't," I said. "I hope you never do."

There was a pause. Music played. Forks scraped plates. A woman laughed.

"I'm sorry to interrupt," I said. "Sounds like you're having a party."

And you said, "Are you okay, Dad?"

"Thanks for sending a check," I said. "I'm grateful."

When we hung up is when I reached for my gun. A hundred dollars wasn't going to solve anything. In a few days, I'd need another hundred. My license plates were expired, I had no car insurance, my phone bill was three months behind, and I couldn't afford the gas to get to the Savannah VA clinic. Earlier that day, I'd emptied my one-gallon Lord Calvert bottle of saved up pocket change to buy two frozen pizzas and a pint of bourbon. So yes, I was in a serious funk.

But the problem with your little story is that you're in too much of a damn hurry for me to shoot myself. You must believe I've always been poor. You know, your mother married me because I was talented and ambitious. A month into our marriage (after I lost my license) she drove me door to door so I could sell vacuums. Three months later, I was managing the office and training the salesmen, *and* taking business courses at the community college. Six years after that (three years after your Mom left and four years after I graduated from the Dale Carnegie Institute), I was sharing a stage with U.S. Presidents. Where the hell is that story?

The college president had hired me as PR director after I graduated, so it was my job, in 1976, to warm up campaign crowds and introduce the candidates. President Ford was arriving by helicopter—so when I saw one approaching, I whipped the crowd into a frenzy to welcome him. It was the wrong heli-copter. His campaign staff was leading the way. And the crowd deflated. But I revived them, kept them energized, and by the time President Ford's helicopter landed, they were louder than before. Afterward, President Ford wrote me this letter: *Your cha-risma was most appreciated on this exhausting campaign trail. If my stay in the White House should get extended and you find yourself in need of a position, please let me know.* A month later, a newspaper photographer shot a picture of Governor Reagan (campaigning for Ford) with his arm around my shoulder, looking up at me. I know you've seen it. Reagan wanted me to move to California to work for *him.* I had my picture taken with Carter, but I never framed it. Point is: I was once on course for a successful life.

Soon after that, the Carolina Eye Bank recruited me (with a hell of a raise, believe me) to head-up their PR department. I flew across the country giving speeches and raising money. I booked Ray Charles, Stevie Wonder, and Ronnie Milsap for a charity concert, but they pulled out after I got fired. Why do people defeat themselves? I hope you never have to ask yourself this question. Two decades blurred by. I drank, my second wife divorced me, my mother died, I drank, ran for public office, forgave my father, remarried, lost the election to a crooked incumbent, my father died, I sold (*a lot* of) real estate, got divorced, remarried, drank, became an award-winning auctioneer, divorced, remarried, drank, divorced, owned my own business (which was very successful very briefly), remarried, poked a needle into my stomach four times a day, drank, divorced, moved.

What I'm saying is that I've been reaching for that gun for thirty years. And if you give one good shit about the truth, you should include this in your story: I lost my stomach for sales. I spent entire days driving around south Georgia and north Florida (paying for my own gas), tracking down leads provided by an art instruction correspondence school. I went to trailer parks and government housing complexes and followed dirt roads deep into the woods. When I saw how these people lived, I didn't have the heart to hard-sell anyone. You made it seem like I was pressuring people to make bad choices. You portrayed me as deluding a single mother into believing that her retarded kid was going to be the next Van Gogh. Your story is dishonest. When I was younger, sure—I persuaded people to spend what they couldn't afford on what they didn't need. And it would still come easy for me—I've been the best salesman everywhere I worked—but I came to realize, while selling art instruction, that I could not sell something I didn't believe in. And since there was nothing I believed in (except for final expense insurance), I saw no point in selling anything.

For three months, I managed a topless restaurant off I-95. Your mother called me the boob boss. It was a sleazy joint and I hated every second of it: 7 p.m. to 7 a.m., baby-sitting the girls. If it looked like one girl got special treatment, other girls accused me of getting special favors. What you imply, again, is dishonest. I promise you—I never laid a hand on any of them. I spent most of my time in the kitchen, dropping frozen patties on the grill. My diabetic feet couldn't tolerate standing for twelve hours at a time, so I walked out one night at midnight, just as two girls got into a hair-pulling fight over a table of cash-waving men. The owners still haven't paid me what they owe me. Three days later I was standing behind a convenience store counter. You should appreciate the pride-swallowing this required, since I once *owned* a convenience store, "Grand Central Station," but I did *not*, as you suggest, inform every customer of this fact. I told no one. Believe me, I've heard enough of those kinds of stories to know how pitiful they sound.

I drove a cab for a week after that, mostly for dope-heads who popped the door and ran, sticking me with the fare. And yes, some crazy man stuck a knife against my neck and got all the money I had, including seven dollars from my own wallet, but there was no dialogue like the kind you must've gotten from television. There was no talking. I took the cab back to my boss and left it. He said I owed him for that night's fare. I told him to kiss my ass and then went home. I was more depressed than ever. I started to understand—I mean *really* understand how desperate some people get, and I started thinking of doing something desperate myself.

So I called you. An hour after that, I was staring at the end of a gun. No offense, but I couldn't think of a single reason not to shoot myself. So I took my gun and drove down to the Winn Dixie and parked in the alley behind the store.

I said, "Goodnight, Irene," and it made me laugh. I told you about her—Miss America, but you don't believe how close I came to moving with her to Lake Tahoe. We attended high school together in Asheville and met again at our 40th class reunion. Even though I didn't graduate, the organizers sent me an invitation, so I said what the hell, maybe I'd sell some final expense insurance. And she came up to *me*, said she remembered me from my night shift as a rock-n-roll DJ, 1957–58. We talked all night, danced, traded phone numbers, met after that in Charleston for two different weekends. She's a classy and intelligent lady and we liked talking to each other. And she's humble—one time I asked a waitress if she had any idea who she was serving, and Irene asked me never to do that again.

When I confessed the truth about my finances, Irene broke it off. I don't blame her. You slandered her as a shallow person, but that's unfair. She was used to a certain standard of success, and I didn't measure up. How would she have introduced me to her friends? How would I talk about my life to them? I wish her well. But sure, I was heartbroken. For a while, I imagined I might live out the rest of my life closer to how I envisioned it forty years before.

It was a clear and soft night, not raining and thundering, the way your story had it. It is true about the putrid smell of grease coming from the Winn Dixie Deli—at least you got that detail right—there was also the smell of rotting garbage coming from the dumpster ten feet away. After a couple minutes, I pulled up to the dumpster and threw the gun into it. Then I reached into the glovebox for my other gun, and tossed it in the dumpster too. I didn't stumble upon any epiphany about the value of life, nor did I think of any good reason for living. I just knew I wasn't thinking too well, and I didn't trust myself with guns. In your story, classical music was playing while I shot myself. But there was no music. In fact, the radio in my Chrysler stopped working four years ago, about the time my air conditioner quit.

I know there's some rule about a gun going off at the end if it shows up at the beginning, but if the story had ended with me shooting myself, it wouldn't be much of a story, if you ask me. That's too easy of an ending. Where you really screwed up is leaving off what happened the next day. "What happened next?" Isn't that supposed to be the main question?

The next afternoon, I was reading the classifieds from Jude's morning newspaper, and I saw where the police department was buying guns off the street for fifty bucks each, no questions asked. Nice timing, right? Story of my life. I went back to the dumpster. No one was around, so I pulled my car right up against it, climbed on the hood and looked over the top down into it. It was about half full, and I couldn't see much except for bags and boxes and scattered shit, so I swung my leg over the top and climbed down in there. You ever been inside a dumpster? I wouldn't recommend it. Two dozen flavors of shit. I moved it all around, covered every square inch, gagged a few times at the smells. Couple minutes later, I heard someone open the back door, so I stood up and saw a man carrying out a bag of garbage. He saw me too, and stopped. It was the same man I'd seen inside the store a dozen times putting up groceries. Maybe you've seen him. Stick-skinny man, wears thick glasses that make his eyes look too big, high-water pants, red windbreaker? I'd asked him a few times where to find something your mother had asked me to pick up, and he always led me to it, nearly sprinting, and I'd thank him, and he'd stand there and smile, and I'd thank him again, and he'd smile his rotten-toothed smile again like he'd just saved my life. But just then, while I was in the dumpster, and he was on the other side of it holding a bag of garbage, he didn't recognize me.

He said, "Hey, you ain't supposed to be in there."

I agreed with him. I wasn't supposed to be in there

"But people do throw away some interesting things, don't they? You won't believe what I found in there this morning."

I already believed it.

"I found two guns in there, and both of them was loaded with bullets." He nodded, persuading me.

I put my forearms on the side of the dumpster and looked above his head toward the sky, bright blue and soft—pleasant for December.

"You won't believe what else?" he said.

I knew what was coming

"I took them to the police station and they gave me a hundred dollars. I was just going to turn them in, you know, in case they was murder weapons. I told them I'd found them in a dumpster, and they said it was my lucky day. You believe that?"

I believed it. I watched a few sea gulls swirl above the dumpster and waited for one of them to drop a shit-ball into my eye.

The guy said, "I got it right here in my pocket." Then he pulled out the money and waved it at me, laughing without any sound coming out.

He said, "I figured I'd go to the Jacksonville flea market. Somebody's got a big truck down there full of cheap movies."

I looked past the sea gulls toward the sky, thinking that some years from now this might be funny. Just then, it wasn't funny at all. I looked back at the man with the thick glasses whose eyes were too big. I said, "You guys hiring?"

He said, "You'd have to talk to Richard about that. You want me to get him?"

"No," I told him. At first I thought I should go home and take a shower, change clothes, come back ready for an interview. Then I looked at this man and thought better of it. "Maybe you could just lead me to him," I said.

So I climbed out of the dumpster, brushed myself off, and followed the guy through the back door, past a kid wrapping grapes, and down the dairy aisle to the manager's office. When we got there, Richard wasn't in. The assistant manager gave me an application.

My new friend said, "You can use me as a reference. Name's Lonnie. L-o-n-n-i-e. I live over yonder." He pointed to the frozen food aisle. Then he shook my hand and walked off.

I went back to my car and drove home. Your mother was moving all of her flowers inside because it was supposed to freeze that night, so I helped her carry them. Probably a hundred damn plants. When we finished, she asked if I was hungry. She'd made too much soup, she said. We sat at her table and talked of how we looked forward to your visit, and how we hoped you'd have more success with your first marriage than we had with ours. Then your mother asked me to promise her something.

"Please," she said. "Do not offer our child any advice about relationships or money."

It was an easy promise to make.

When you did come home, I was happy to see you. I was happy we got to talk alone one night. I told you this story that you made into your own version. But it reminds me now of what my father said whenever someone told a story that he suspected was mostly bullshit. He'd say, "Nothing ruins a good story like an eyewitness," and then he'd be off and running with his own version of the story he claimed to know better because he'd seen it himself, but his version was mostly bullshit too.

So, I don't mean to ruin your story—it's your business to tell it the way you want to, and I realize that you're young and you're still learning, so screwing up is a natural part of the process. I hope the next time you're home, we can talk about endings. I want to sit in the condo facing each other in my fine plastic furniture, and I want to ask whether you could imagine a story that ends more painfully because the hero continues living. Then I'll pour us another round and tell you this story again.

Clarissa Drives John-Boy to the Jacksonville Airport

Your whole damn family think I'm crazy because I can't stop talking, all the time saying I must have an *affliction*, but I say it's a blessing, like the way some people is born with the god-given talent to sing and all they can do is sing, and all they *should* do is sing because it hurts *not* to sing and if they stop singing they might die because they got so much stuff boiling up inside them it's *got* to come out all at once or they'll explode or either kill somebody, which is how I feel *all* the time, except I can't sing, damn it. I can't sing.

After I started taking your grandmama to church I went up to Father Ted one day and I said, "Father Ted? What do I need to do to *convert?*" You know what he said? He said, "Stop singing so loud." He said the choir had complained that I was throwing them off and drowning them out. Your poor grandmama, I must've made her half-deaf singing in the pew next to her, but she never once said any mean thing to me about anything, except sometimes at home late in the afternoon when we'd be sitting around after our programs and I'd be talking and talking, she'd say, "Clarissa—it's time to say your Mary prayers." Oh Jesus, I'm gonna miss that woman. You see what I did with the car keys? Okay. Alright. Here we go.

If I didn't have to ride back by myself, I'd drive you all the way to North damn-Dakota so I could tell you my *whole* life story and you'd find out how I survived this long. All you going to get this morning is a few *snippets*. I went to Minnesota thirty years ago. Didn't see *no* black people. This nun hired me to go there and get her mama and bring her back because that nun didn't like to drive but I love to drive, so me and that nun and that nun's mama, we all rode back together and we got along real well. That nun's mama, she talked as much as I did. I'd talk for thirty minutes, then she'd talk for thirty minutes and we went back and forth like that for two days. I love to *go*. When it came time for me to pick professions, I should've gotten my CDL license and drove a truck.

I thought your grandmama's funeral was nice. But it was so quiet. Just a few sniffles here and there. You know she gave me this car? You should see all the looks I get driving back through my neighborhood with Jesus stuck up there on the dashboard. I told her I'd pay her something for it, that she could keep a week's pay at least, but she told me to shut up. My own mama was bat-shit crazy—I'm talking about the kind of crazy who rubs shit in her own hair kind of crazy. You never seen crazy like that, and I pray you never do. Why your family call you John-boy? It's after that character on the TV show who wears those silly round glasses like you're wearing? And he was trying to be a writer too, right? I never liked that show. We could only pick up one channel about half the time. And you get *paid* to tell people how to write they stories? You need to get me up there in that classroom to tell some stories. Except not in the winter time. *I* got sense enough to stay out that kind of damn cold.

You look *nervous*. Am I going too fast? In my previous life I was a race car driver and I probably died in a race car wreck, because I like to go fast. Sometimes I just be cruising along, daydreaming about everything I done been through, and I look down and see that speedometer needle sitting on 95. I don't mean to scare nobody. Your poor grandmama, I probably pushed her in the grave *prematurely*, but she never criticized my driving. She told me she'd gotten a ticket in her time. And she told me about all the trouble you got into while she was raising you up and all the troubles you done had in your adult life trying to keep a woman and a job while you move all around the country trying to find yourself or whatever, and how she kept loving you even when you went a long while without calling or writing, and you might not believe this right now when you in the darkest bit of the night right before the dawn, but you got to let your regrets go and get on with making the most of the little-bitty time you got left.

But it's hard. Here I am thinking, damn, I should've been a truck driver. I got to let that go. Then I start thinking about what-all else I could've done with my life and how coming up out of Tarboro without getting no further than Woodbine until I was seventeen years old made me ignorant of what was out there to even *be* dreaming about, except for being a cook or a maid or a teacher. We couldn't even see any TV shows to make us a*ware* that they was other things to dream about. You ever been to Tarboro? Get on Highway 17 going south, you'll see Waverly, then you'll see a little town called White Oak, and you take 252 going to Folkston and after you pass White Oak, they's about four pine trees and then in Tarboro they's about maybe eight houses and then you go on down and you'll be in Jerusalem and then you'll be in Red Cap and then you'll be—Sand Hill don't go that way, Sand Hill branches off—but then after Red Cap you'll be almost to Folkston. Now, they call it Burnt Fort Road. And so then I think about what could've happened if I hadn't spent all my growing-up years working at those juke joints, one in Tarboro called The Ponderosa and one in Woodbine called The Brown Derby. The Brown Derby still standing. Oh Jesus. I think those places has something to do with my phobia of not being able to shut up. I remember being there when I was a infant, and then I started serving alcohol when I was five years old. My god-daddy, he owned The Ponderosa. Lots of people came in there to dance and carry on, but I never was allowed to dance. I made the sandwiches, served the sandwiches, served the liquor, served the beer, and made more sandwiches. It was child labor *and* abuse. I didn't get paid. When I got hungry I had to buy my own sandwiches except for sometimes the ladies who was there—the ladies of the *night*—they'd buy theyself a sandwich and give me half, then they'd go back and do what they did with the married men who came in there. Every night, my uncle and my god-daddy picked up the drunks and toted them out the door and laid them on the ground. My god-daddy, he's buried beneath the front step. Why would you want to be buried like that, beneath the front step of a place where drunk people could keep walking all over you? I never understood that. But they got it okayed in the county, and that's where he's buried, beneath the front step. That alcohol turns people into *devils*. Do you still drink? You look hungover right now, be honest with you. I never liked it. To this day if I get a whiff of it, I get sick to my stomach. What time your plane take off? I might ought to speed up a little bit.

It was drunks and kin was all I *knew* growing up. Drunks and kin. When I was sixteen and in eleventh grade, I thought I might be escaping out of it, because I went to work for my aunt who bought a club in Woodbine, and I liked that club because Woodbine was *new* to me. Plus it was prettier young boys in Woodbine than it was in Tarboro. That's the other thing you learn—every time you think you escaping, you really just swapping the *devil for the witch*. Then I hit that tail-chasing age that leads to more regrets. Who you loved that didn't love you; who loved you that you didn't love; whose heart did you break to pieces and who broke yours? Then you pick the wrong person to marry and half your damned life is over and you facing the other half wondering whether you ever going to laugh again. Got to let it go. I can't even stand to think about all that—it would drive me crazy. Got to let it go.

The first pretty boy I met in Woodbine lived next door to the Brown Derby—a *handsome* man named Bruce Winston who I took to be my boyfriend. And do you know he wanted to marry me? He was serious, but I wasn't serious—I *had* a boyfriend, Caleb Flowers, who was in Vietnam. I always had at least two boyfriends. I never believed in putting all my eggs into a *single* basket. I had another boyfriend then too, Calvin Rose. There was Calvin Rose, Caleb Flowers, and Bruce Winston. And I had one more man down the street who liked me, but I ain't have time for no more than three. You okay? You going to make it? Crack that window a little bit. You look pale. There you go. I took Bruce from my cousin Mattie. Everybody told him not to leave that good girl to come play with somebody who didn't want him. But he didn't *know* I didn't want him, see. And then he was about to leave to go to college over at the Tuskegee *Institute* and wanted me to go with him, but I wasn't about to follow no man *nowhere*. And I still had my eyes on Caleb Flowers and Calvin Rose. You talk about a good-looking man? Calvin Rose was handsome. I never messed around with no *ugly* man. And even Steve—you met Steve at the funeral—when we first dated, he looked just *like* Teddy Pendergrass. But I had ugly-man friends, now, and all of them liked me too, because I paid attention to them and talked to them, but they knew they didn't have no chance with such a nice-looking well-shaped woman like myself. Oh, Jesus. Then I had another boyfriend when I went to college, Theodore Carter, he was studying to be—what was he studying to be? I don't know. But he was the smartest man at Brunswick Junior College. Everybody went to him to get help with they lesson—help with geometry and help with biology, everything. Theodore Carter was a damn *book*worm. But he would never get fresh or touch me—he was too much of a gentleman. I didn't *want* no gentleman. I wanted somebody who was going to put they *arms* around me. Or somebody who at least would *try* to touch me, even if I said, *no*, I don't want to be touched right now. You done been married how many times? Are you too much of a gentleman? That might be one of your problems. A woman wants a man who will show some affection. And then Theodore Carter up and said to me, he said, "Clarissa, will you marry me?" and I said, "Theodore Carter I don't *love* you," and he said, "Oh Clarissa, just *fool* me." I said I couldn't fool him. You know from that time to this time, we're still friends, and he's got a wife and I've got Steve, but whenever he see me in church—my home-church—he'll come up to me and say, "Clarissa, be my girlfriend." He told me he was looking for a girlfriend who was younger than 45 and less than 200 pounds, that asshole. I reminded him I was married. He said, "Can't you handle two?" I said I could handle two, three, or four, but I didn't *want* to. I told him I was *happily* married, but he looked at me like I was speaking in tongues, so I just pushed him out my way and went on. But I guess that means I still got it. Don't you think I still got it?

I don't know what make two people stay together. When I met Steve, my soul was in the lost and found, like Aretha say, then he came along and *claimed* it, made me feel like a *natural* woman. But you know what he really did? He made me feel special enough to let me know I didn't really need nobody. That's what made me fall in love with him. And he appreciates everything I done been through and he likes that I'm a strong woman. Of course, he got his own house out behind our house, so that helps too. He fixed up the garage like a little a*part*ment—got him a TV out there and a refrigerator, a couch. He put a new steel door on it after I kicked in the old one. He go out there and lock his door when he get home from work so he can relax, and he keep it locked when I go pound on it and scream for him to let me in. Hell, if I was married to me, I might need a separate house too. Maybe that's what every couple need. I don't know. You look a little green. You going to make it? If you're going to be sick, let me know—I'll slam on the brakes and put you out. I can't have nobody getting sick in my new car.

When I met Steve is when I stopped being quiet. I was shy for a long while, believe it or not. But one morning I woke up and I said, you know what? I'm going to express myself now. That was 1968. Before that, when I was quiet, more people liked me. But when I started talking, people liked me *less*. Why is that? And why didn't I *care*? Crack that window some more.

Here come the little ol' town of Woodbine. Hello Woodbine. Bye-bye Woodbine. You take that road and go down and back and there's one-two-three-four-five little buildings and that's it. It's a Laundromat, it's a "we sell dead people things" place, a post office, a bank, and a video place. Smaller than Mayberry. They did build a courthouse. *Big* courthouse. You got to go all the way up to St. Mary's to get to a hospital. They got a clinic—a little ol' doctor's office like they got in those villages across the way. It's a little building where a doctor comes in from out of town. And I think they got a dentist now. No *Mac*-Donald's, no Burger King. We used to have a place—it was a one room place where you could get a hamburger and a milkshake. Called it The Georgia Girl.

In 1968 is when I taught Calvin Rose how to kiss. He was *so* handsome. But he didn't know nothing. I mean, *nothing*. I bet that boy appreciates me still today for what I taught him. You know who taught me to kiss? Herschel Clements. He was twenty-one and I was fifteen. Herschel Clements taught me and I taught Calvin Rose. But that's all I taught Calvin. I wasn't about to give up the cookies for Calvin Rose, even if he was the handsomest man around. Calvin Rose wanted me to marry him and so did Bruce Winston and so did Caleb Flowers—and Caleb, he the one who maybe, maybe, *maybe* I would've married. I don't know. He was the first one proposed to me, but he was about to go to Vietnam and I was *young*. I didn't know much, but I *knew* I wasn't ready to marry nobody and start having babies. I had already been helping my aunt at her house and I hated her little babies and I hated changing they diapers—back then they ain't have no Pampers. Can you imagine *that*? Jesus. But Caleb Flowers. I loved him for a short while and shipped him off to Vietnam and then for a little while I was playing with Bruce next door and there was also Anthony Antoine Atkins. *That* was a nice looking man. He thought I was going to marry him, and he *was* handsome, but his eyes was too big. My eyes was al*ready* big. You think I was going to marry him? Don't you know if we'd had a child, its big eyes would be sitting up on its little head like a frog's eyes? And then Big Mac Copeland came along—*he* was good-looking. One night, Big Mac Copeland put the moves on me like no other man has *ever* put the moves on me—oh, did he put the moves on *me*. He was about to propose to me too, but then he got his hands blown off at that Thiokol hand grenade plant in Woodbine when they had that explosion there in 1971. Couple my cousins was working there too, a few of my friends—it was about thirty people died, probably 29 of them was black people. I bet you weren't even alive yet. Look at it on the internet. Thiokol plant in Woodbine. They made flares and hand grenades and stuff like that to send to Vietnam. Jimmy Carter flew in on his helicopter from the Governor's mansion. All the woods around there caught fire too. One of my second cousins, Bill Sprawley, Jr? Both his mama *and* his wife died in that explosion, then round-about two weeks later, his little baby died of a heart attack. I didn't know infants could have heart attacks, but that's what the doctor said it was. Billy disappeared after that. He was a *young* man, just out of high-school-young. The families sued the plant and the government for not labeling the right things as *explosive*, and they won, but it took twenty years before anybody got any money. Big Mac Copeland lost his hands. Other people come running out the building on fire, pieces of burning metal in they backs or around they heads. Whole town was devastated. It's a memorial plaque there now. You know where Waverly is? You turn right at Jake's place—that's my god-brother place right there—that's a branch off that juke joint from Tarboro—I go over there and look at that place and I'd rather spit than to stop—but you go there and after you turn left then you turn right and it's a little park where they got a plaque with all the ones who died in that Thiokol explosion. I thank God I was smart enough not to let my aunt talk me into going to work there like she tried so hard to do, 'cause you know I would've been dead? And oh Jesus what the world would've missed.

You don't have no siblings, do you? If you feel alone in this world, let me tell you something: having siblings is no guarantee that you won't be alone. Me and my sister got separated. Not at birth. She was in 7th grade and I was in 5th grade, and she went to live with my rich uncle in Washington D.C. who was a big-shot supervisor at that big hospital there—what's it called, Walter-somebody? Reed. She went up there and I stayed here with my poor Indian grandmama in Tarboro. But you know what? I think I got the better raising. Because the things that go across my sister's brain? I don't know. She always talking about how she got no reason to go on living. I look at her and I say how in the *devil* did you get like this? She got all kinds of book-smarts, but she can't even drive. And she can't leave home unless she carry a list. She *sure* can't go to the grocery store unless she carry a list. I *know* what I need. I need eggs and milk and Kleenex and toilet paper. She's got two masters degrees *and* a PhD. Went to school all her life. I enrolled in Brunswick Junior College and maybe I should've kept going, but I fell in love with Teddy damned Pendergrass and started having babies. Difference between me and my sister is that she had some help, and I didn't have no help. And I ended up a stronger person. Maybe I should've gotten some book-smarts, but I had to work forty hours a week *and* go to school *and* study and I had a husband and a baby and a old jalopy-Plymouth that broke down about every two miles. I got tired of listening to people trying to teach me things I ain't have time to think about. But my sister? I don't understand her. Once you retire, wouldn't you get you a hobby or go work somewhere or do something just to kill some time? She don't do nothing except sit around and be miserable. Matter a fact, after she retired, she sold her house and left her children and her grandchildren and her friends and came to live with *me*! Ain't something wrong with that? The way she was raised made her crazy in a different way. She always had it easy. She had it made on a *flowerbed* of ease. She must've thought I could help her. Why else she want to come live with *me*? But she beyond my help. I mean she had some drama, but her drama was different from my drama. Crack that window some more. I know you can't help it.

When I was eighteen, my family talked me into getting on a bus and going up there to see her. My uncle, he promised me a job making forty-five dollars a week—lotta money in 1968. What I saw when I got there made me want to turn right around and come back home. We can go this way—the Pecan Park exit, but I'm going to take the next exit. Oh Jesus. My uncle had four boys, but they took her in as the girl they didn't have. And the boys they used to wrestle and fight and one day all of them decided they was going to beat *her* up. And by the time my uncle got home that day, she was sitting on the front step crying. But my uncle, he didn't beat up all the boys. Here, the way *we* was raised up—one person do something wrong, *everybody* get they ass tore up. But up there, he only beat up one of the boys for beating her up. And after he beat that boy, his wife got mad, and she started abusing my sister. By abuse, I mean she made her clean and cook and wash they clothes, wait on them hand and foot. She wouldn't let her be a majorette, wouldn't let her be in the band—wouldn't let her do nothing. Soon as she finish school every day, she rushed home and started cleaning. And my sister so easily brainwashed, she did this all her life until I went up there—and then they made me take over for her. Come to find out, that's what my new job was. I went from spending all my spare time with my boyfriends—I was eighteen years old and out of high school—to staying cooped up in they house with one-two-three-four locks on *one* door. I felt like I was confined in the institution. I had to clean the bathroom upstairs, the bathroom in the middle and the bathroom in the basement seven days a week. Meanwhile, my sister, she start sitting around the house entertaining her ditty-ass friends while my uncle's wife working the hell out of *me*. I felt like Cindafucking*rella*. I didn't like my job back at Tarboro, but at least I got to keep all my money there. My uncle's wife, she always kept fifteen dollars out my weekly pay for herself. See? I swapped the devil for the witch. But I wrote Caleb Flowers a letter—my boyfriend in Vietnam. I wrote him and told him to propose marriage to me because I had to get the hell out that house. I told him just how to write the letter. And when he wrote me and asked me to marry him, I showed that letter to my uncle and he said, yeah, okay. See they was looking at that military check from Vietnam while Caleb Flowers over there getting his ass wiped out. And I told my uncle I had to go home and get ready for my wedding because Caleb Flowers was coming home at such and such a date and my uncle said, "I'll take you." And I told everybody I was getting married, but all I was doing was getting the hell out of Washington D.C. My sister told me later, she said, "I wish I had been that smart." And I told her, I said—you dumbass, we came from the same mama, and you got *no* brains! Jesus. And then all those many years later, after she retired, she came to live with me because she wanted me to nurse all her emotional problems. But I had my own stuff I wanted to get done and she demanded constant attention, so finally I decided to turn the tables on her and drive her crazy so she'd leave. Before I let somebody drive me crazy, I drive them crazy first. That's the secret, right there. And one day she told me in her goody-two-shoes way, she said, "Clarissa, I must leave now and search for a peaceful place to live." So I opened the door for her and told her ass goodbye and good luck. Then she moved to Atlanta, which was good, but she's not doing any better. It don't matter where she live or who she live with, she's going to be crazy. I guess I should go see her. She might be in a mental institution by now, which is where our mama died.

I'll follow this sign says *departing*.

My mama got sent to the mental institution in Milledgeville when I was two weeks old. They tried to tell me I drove her crazy, but they didn't know what they was talking about back then. That was 1950. They took me to see her when I was in the fifth grade. They pointed to a strange lady rocking in a rocking chair over in the corner and they said "Clarissa, that's your mama." Now, why would you do a child like that? See, they the ones who made me all mixed up. I'm not responsible for being mixed up. They did that to me. They point to a strange lady sitting in the corner and say there's your mama, but she ain't meant nothing to me. She ain't meant *nothing* to me. I'm in fifth grade and all I know is my grandmama, just like all you knew was your grandmama. How you gonna feel when somebody take you to a mental institution for one day and point to a strange lady and say there's your mama? How you gonna feel?

One time about a year after that, when I was in sixth grade, they went to get her and brought her back to my grandmama house. And she was sitting down eating some fried fish so fast— this is when I *knew* she was crazy—she was eating that fish with her hands so fast me and my grandmama had to stand back and just stare at her, and my grandmama was laughing, but it wasn't funny. And later that same day, I remember my mama chasing my cousin Jill and some of my other cousins—chasing them around the yard trying to get a doll they was keeping away from her. Then they took her back that afternoon, and I never saw her again. She never meant nothing to me. But I should go see my sister. How is it some people end up okay and some people don't? You flying Delta? I'm gonna pull up here.

You going to make it? Is they any good food up there? I should've made you something to carry with you. You gonna be okay. When you coming back? You let me know. Seriously. Let me know. I'll pick you up. You better take a Kleenex. Just let me know. Better take another one.

Oh sweet Jesus Lord God have mercy, who I'ma talk to on the way home? I might have to say my Mary prayers and talk to the *plastic* Jesus. I know what I'll do—I'll sing myself home. I'll be alright. Go on now, before you miss that plane.

What?

Stop that.

You mean to tell me after all I done told you about everything I done been through, you too scared to get out this car?

Okay. Alright, yeah, give me a hug.

Okay.

You're welcome.

Alright. Yeah. Okay, honey.

You're welcome.

Okay. Alright. Here we go.

You're welcome.

Any Idiot Can Feel Pain

FROM: brightside7@hotmail.com
TO: dominiquejd@ekcc.edu
DATE: Mon, Sep 30, 1:35 a.m.
SUBJECT: Gratitude (with an invitation!)

Dear Professor Dom,

Six months ago, my twenty-year-old daughter, Gabriella, was afraid to leave our house, but I'm writing now to thank you for making your televised classes available at the library because I believe they have saved her life. She prefers not to watch your face, but she loves to hear your voice. When we got the DVD's, she put her father's old tape cassette player next to the TV and recorded your voice, then carried your voice around the house. At night, she leaves it on her bedside table because you help her get to sleep, which I'm eternally grateful for.

Though Gabriella prefers to listen, I have enjoyed watching. My favorite part is when you yank the purple beret off your head and throw it into the waste basket and pour lighter fluid over it and set it on fire, and then right after that, I love how you put on your welding helmet and say "Let's stop dreaming and get to work, people!" (Episode 1). And I laughed when your student-assistant came running out with her fire extinguisher, wearing her safety goggles and toy firefighter's hat, then engulfed you in smoke while you kept talking. Some people might not approve of your methods, but I get the feeling that you don't care, which is something else that makes us love you.

Two years ago from next week, Gabriella's father died from a self-inflicted gunshot wound that came out of nowhere. It happened while Gabriella was in her first month at the state university on a full music scholarship. She plays piccolo. Nine months later is when she suffered her nervous collapse. I've attached a picture of her with our poodle, Carmen. Behind her is a portrait I painted of her father, Bill, who was a roofer. Over Gabriella's other shoulder is a portrait I painted of my mother, now confined to a wheelchair. She never complains and constantly prays to the Virgin Mary for all of us to keep getting better. I took up painting when Bill died. I'm no Picasso, but I stopped caring about "the product" when I heard you say "the process" is much more valuable (Episode 2).

Gabriella's favorite place to listen to you is when she's sitting on the kitchen floor putting together puzzles. The other day, while she worked on a 2,000-piece puzzle of Cinque Terre, Italy, I heard her laughing (such a rare and beautiful sound!) at this quote you attributed to Erica Jong: "Beware of the man who denounces women writers; his penis is tiny and he cannot spell." Another day, we both appreciated the quote from Dorothy . . . I don't remember her last name . . . who said "Fear is a chasm to swallow his (the writer's) hope." I also smiled when you said that Jesus said, "In my Father's house there are many mansions." My other favorite moment is when you interviewed the young man from Lexington who got out of prison and enrolled in college and then decided to devote himself to helping people (Episode 6). I cried at the end when he gave you a hug and thanked you for being such a good role model for him. And then I laughed when you asked him to loan you twenty dollars.

I'm writing in hopes that you might be interested in meeting Gabriella so you can see for yourself how truly special she is. She loves to learn. She looks up things on Wikipedia about great inventors, scientists, musicians, writers, mathematicians, and dancers, and she is constantly asking me to get her books and music from the library. She loves listening to Cecilia Bartoli, the Italian opera star, and she is obsessed with everything by Puccini and Verdi. I get the idea that she is most drawn to Italians as those she admires, which I'm beginning to think has something to do with a previous life, though I'm normally not one to believe such ideas. She also listens to "classes" on the public access channel (imagine—out of all the channels to choose from) and that is how we first found you, though all we saw at that time was the very end, when you present a diploma and a carrot to your student-assistant who looks very bored, though I'm betting you told her to look that way for comic effect (Episode 15).

Do you know Rosa, the math teacher at the college? Gabriella audited one of her online classes. After that class, Rosa called Gabriella once a week and came by our house for regular visits, always bringing a book or a math-related puzzle or game. She was very generous with her time. On her last visit, she brought some of her own Math-Art pieces, which are these wonderfully detailed drawings of lines and shapes that connect in various patterns that "entertain the eye," as Rosa says. She gave Gabriella a piece called "Habitat" and helped us hang it on the ceiling over Gabriella's bed. Gabriella's confidence soared under Rosa's tutelage, reaching a peak three weeks ago when she left the house and walked out to the mailbox. But that came to a crashing halt yesterday, when Rosa called from Barcelona to tell us she was taking a year off to travel across Europe before beginning a new job in

Montreal. She apologized to Gabriella for not being able to tell her in person that she was moving. Gabriella handed me the phone and went to her room and started crying, leaving me to talk to Rosa. She said she'd divorced her husband and left the country just to get away from him. She said it had been a hard year. I told her I knew something about hard years. Gabriella spent the rest of that day in bed, staring at Rosa's "Habitat" while she listened to your voice. She did not respond to *my* voice or my mother's voice at all, refusing meals, rebuffing every attempt at consolation. I lay on the floor to keep her company while you talked about so many things, like the difference between coherence and unity. One part she kept rewinding was when you played your bongo drums very loudly (and very badly!) just before you talked about dependent clauses and independent clauses and conjunctions and semicolons and how we should use all four sentence types (1. simple 2. compound 3. complex 4. compound-complex) in various sequences so we'd be "less monotonous-sounding than professors." She also liked when you talked about using punctuation (or no punctuation) like music notation. She stared at the ceiling and listened like it was the most fascinating thing she'd ever heard. Without your voice to latch onto, I think she'd still be in bed, grieving over Rosa's departure.

This might seem like a weird question since we've never met (but you never know without asking, right?), but we were wondering if you would be interested in attending Gabriella's birthday party this October 10 (a birthday she shares with Giuseppe Verdi, b. 1813 in Le Roncone, Italy), at 6 p.m. I'll make her favorite dish, eggplant parmesan, a specialty of mine, my secret being to select the most purple eggplants completely free of bruises and to add roasted garlic and caramelized onions and dry bread crumbs, and to salt, dry, and drain each piece prior to cooking; this removes the bitterness and causes the eggplant slices to "sweat," which reduces the water content and results in less oil absorption. If you don't like eggplant, I can modify.☺

You probably get many requests like this from strangers who have certain ideas about you because you're on television, but my invitation has nothing to do with wanting to "rub elbows" with the famous. After all, "Fame means that millions of people have the wrong idea of who you are" (Erica Jong, Episode 15). Frankly, I think meeting Gabriella could do *you* some good, Dr. Dom. I have a secret. I've seen you in the grocery store, and it always shocks me to see how sad you look while you're trying to pick out the right cantaloupe. (Helpful hint: try sniffing them to see if you get a sweet flowery-type smell, then squeeze them to make sure they're not rock-hard, look for a golden/orange-type color on the rind, then give it a knock to check for a "dull thud." If they're all too green, get one and leave it on the counter a few days but make sure it's not too soft, which means it's overripe). I've seen you slink around the store with your head down and shoulders sagging from some kind of sorrow you don't want to burden your viewers with. Then you always perk up in the checkout line. You smile at the cashier and say something that makes him/her smile, along with the bagboy/girl. Then you walk slowly across the parking lot, get in your old Toyota (identical to what Bill drove, btw!) and go home to your upstairs apartment which is always dark because you turn on the light and close the curtains, which makes me think you must be lonely.

Please don't misunderstand: I'm no stalker. I only know where you live because it happens to be in the same direction I take home from the grocery store, but please believe me: I have been very careful to respect your privacy and I have no intention of invading it. Maybe I'm completely wrong, but I think that someone with your gifts for being such an inspiration to so many people might also benefit from being shown some appreciation every once in a blue moon. If you could see Gabriella's face while she is listening to you, it would recharge your enthusiasm and renew your sense of purpose for doing the good work you do, which maybe is something you don't get to hear too often.

I suppose I'm not doing so well with being "concise," which is what you say good writers are good at (Episode 14.) I apologize for any grammatical errors or improper language usage. I have written this letter carefully and painstakingly over several days with countless revisions and I have proofread it many times, but I am no professional like you, and I feel like I should send this now because to keep piddling would just be another form of procrastination, right? But please don't feel any pressure. If we don't hear from you, it's perfectly fine. Really. I just wanted you to know that you have already made a very dramatic difference!

Very truly yours,
Susan Gilchrist

p.s. Even a phone call would cheer up Gabriella. Every time the phone rings, her eyes light up thinking it might be Rosa, but it's usually just a doctor's office calling to confirm one of her appointments or one of my mother's appointments or now, one of my own appointments as I'm having some tests to see about chest pains and flagging energy. When Gabriella discovers it's not Rosa, her eyes go dark again. But then she turns to your voice and that gets her through the day. It's a remarkable thing to witness.

FROM: dominiquejd@ekcc.edu
TO: brightside7@hotmail.com
DATE: Mon, Sep 30, 1:35 a.m.
SUBJECT: auto-reply

I'm away on emergency business. For immediate help, contact the English Department.

Yours,
Dom

FROM: brightside7@hotmail.com
TO: dominiquejd@ekcc.edu
DATE: Wed, Oct 2, 1:47 a.m.
SUBJECT: any idiot can feel pain

Dear Dom,

Please disregard my previous email until you have settled the more important matter you are now attending to. In the meantime, I hope you will find it uplifting to know that the only solution to Gabriella's emergency of last night was the sound of your voice. I heard a whimpering/howling from her room, so I went to check, thinking she was having a nightmare, but her eyes were wide open and the first thing she said (after I turned on her light and assured her that no one was outside her window) was, "Dr. Dom." So I played your voice and we both listened while you "put on" your exaggerated German accent and talked about subject/verb agreement, pronoun agreement, parallel sentence structure, ambiguous, misplaced, and dangling modifiers, apostrophes, lie vs. lay, who vs. whom, and which vs. that (Episode 5). What's funny is that I remember how much I enjoyed *watching* this because you got into character with your fake mustache and your army uniform (with one stripe!) and your WWII army helmet and boots and yardstick, but Gabriella truly enjoyed *listening*. Very soon she was sleeping peacefully.

The next morning, she took your voice to the bathroom and listened to you talk about conjugating verbs while she completed her hygiene rituals. When she came out of the bathroom, you were at the end of that episode and were talking about the three P's: Patience, Perseverance and Persistence. I wish the same for you now, Dom. Sometimes I wonder if it's hard for you to remember employing the same techniques that you prescribe to others, so I hope you will put yourself first for a change in order to resolve whatever emergency you're facing. You closed that class with another inspirational quote from Erica Jong, who said, "The trick is not how much pain you feel—but how much joy you feel. Any idiot can feel pain. Life is full of excuses to feel pain, excuses not to live, excuses, excuses, excuses." That's so true isn't it?

Very truly yours,
Susan Gilchrist

p.s. Here's hoping you'll resolve your emergency in time to join us for family fun on Oct. 10!

FROM: dominiquejd@ekcc.edu
TO: brightside7@hotmail.com
DATE: Wed, Oct 2, 1:47 a.m.
SUBJECT: auto-reply

I'm away on emergency business. For immediate help, contact the English Department.

Yours,
Dom

FROM: brightside7@hotmail.com
TO: dominiquejd@ekcc.edu
DATE: Sat, Oct 5, 2:15 a.m.
SUBJECT: punching bags/dancing

Dear Dom,

I wanted to share another example of how you've helped us so it'll make you smile. Yesterday, I took Mom to the doctor, and the report was bad. He said it could be anywhere from a month to a year, which is breaking our hearts. I worry most for Gabriella. Just when she seems to be making progress, I worry that Mom's death would cause a severe setback. But here's the uplifting part: yesterday, Gabriella started playing episode 14, which I remember watching—where you stand next to the punching bag wearing your funny boxing headgear and your boxing shorts pulled up to your armpits and your red boxing gloves and your white tank-top T-shirt and you remove your mouthpiece to talk about metaphors, and how the punching bag is an example of one because it represents a person who takes a beating from all the hardships that keep pounding us over and over in an unrelenting fashion, then you insert your mouthpiece and hit the punching bag several times with your skinny arms and you explain how certain hardships like the death of a loved one will try to knock us out, or if it's not the death of a loved one trying to knock us out it's a cheating spouse teaming up with a custody battle or it's the constant stress that comes with *never* having enough money, or it's the long-term lingering effects of an abusive father you could never please or it's a power-hungry "asshole-boss" who mistreats workers or it's a group of gossip-mongering colleagues, or it's a series of Presidents like Reagan, Bush, and Bush and all their Supreme Court justices who keep pounding away at poor people and women and minorities who have no counter-punching power (you were on quite a roll), and you said we had to be as strong as punching bags and absorb a certain amount of unwarranted punishment and *refuse* to be knocked out, and then you explained the rope-a-dope strategy the David-like Muhammad Ali (who called himself "a boxing scholar" you said) employed to defeat the Goliath-like George Foreman in their 1974 "Rumble in the Jungle" which was Ali's decision to absorb Foreman's punches so he'd be tired when Ali decided it was time to dance, and I must say too that the way you slipped into your Ali impersonation was impressive, I should know, because Bill, who was also from Louisville (like you and

Ali), impersonated him very well too. But Gabriella's favorite part is when you grab your boombox and set it on the stool next to you and start playing Elton John's "I'm Still Standing (yeah, yeah, yeah)." Then you put your mouthpiece back in and punch the bag while the song plays and you raise your skinny arms up over your head and do a little dance while you face the camera and wink. While the song played, I caught Gabriella in the kitchen DANCING with my mother (still in her wheelchair), which was a beautiful sight I wish you could have seen. I'm very grateful to you for that. So, keep on doing the rope-a-dope and keep on standing (yeah, yeah, yeah!). We're in your corner!

Yours,
S.

p.s. I took the liberty of telling Gabriella that I invited you to her birthday party (Oct 10, 6 p.m.). I keep telling her there are no guarantees, that you might already have plans, but she was beside herself with excitement. It's wonderful to see her finally looking forward to something. Just a 5-minute drop-in or even a telephone call could work a miracle.

FROM: dominiquejd@ekcc.edu
TO: brightside7@hotmail.com
DATE: Sat, Oct 5, 2:15 a.m.
SUBJECT: auto-reply

I'm away on emergency business. For immediate help, contact the English Department.

Yours,
Dom

FROM: brightside7@hotmail.com
TO: dominiquejd@ekcc.edu
DATE: Mon, Oct 7, 11:55 p.m.
SUBJECT: courage

Dear Dom,

Maybe you're still absorbing punches from your emergency issue. Or maybe procrastination temporarily has you against the ropes. It's always a battle isn't it? I'm writing to give you an encouraging update on Gabriella, which is that today she went to the mailbox again. What allowed her to do it, I'm convinced, is that she carried your voice with her. You were talking about courage (Episode 7). You said to commit words to a page required courage and that every human being had enough courage inside herself to do it. You confessed that there were often days in your own life when it required plenty of courage just to get out of bed, eat breakfast, take a shower, put on clothes, leave the house, go somewhere, speak to someone. This is when Gabriella walked out to the street in her pajamas to get the mail. It was seven a.m. and too early, but she wasn't even discouraged that nothing was there. She came back inside and took your voice to the living room, put on a CD of Luciano Pavarotti performing Nessun dorma from Puccini's *Turandot*, and she also put in a DVD documentary on Renaissance Art, though she muted the TV and just watched the paintings and sculptures (Michelangelo was featured prominently, of course), and she turned down Pavarotti enough to keep listening to you (her recorder was in her lap) while you talked about the courage it takes to write a one-page resume, and the greater courage still that it takes to send that resume out to a hundred places and the courage it takes above that *to wait* "without hope and without despair" (Isak Dinesen) for results that may or may not pay off. I just wanted to share this news right away with someone, and I could think of no one more appropriate than you, since you have meant so much to Gabriella. Very truly yours,

S.

p.s. Oct. 10 is fast approaching. If you can manage to come, please don't feel any pressure to bring anything. Your presence alone would be the most meaningful gift for Gabriella.

FROM: postmaster@mail.hotmail.com (postmaster@mail.hotmail.com)
TO: brightside7@hotmail.com
DATE: Mon, Oct 7, 11:56 p.m.
SUBJECT: Delivery Status Notification (Failure)

This is an automatically generated Delivery Status Notification.

Delivery to the following recipients failed.

dominiquejd@ekcc.edu

8 October
Dominique Adagio
113 Gentry St. Apt. 23

Dear Dom,

I got worried, so I went to the college to find you. I was also still clinging to some hope that I could persuade you to attend Gabriella's birthday party. I went up and down the halls looking for your name on all the doors, but I couldn't find it. Then I went to the English Department and met an unpleasant man wearing a purple beret (ha-ha, I imagined it on fire!) who told me you no longer worked there. Then he said he was late for a meeting and scampered off with an ugly frown.

So I went to the department secretary, a nice woman named Sue, who told me everything. She said at the end of the semester's first week, you stepped from her boss's office and handed her your keys and said, in a child's pouty voice, "I quit." She thought you were joking, but then she said you called yourself "A fraud." Why would you call yourself that, Dom? Then she told me how just a couple of months ago your wife (a math professor at the college!) left you and moved away. I should have made this connection sooner. I'm so sorry. Still, the fact that Rosa once loved you only increases my respect for you, because I know Rosa chooses wisely the people she devotes herself to. And the week after Rosa left you is when, according to Sue, your colleagues voted against giving you tenure, apparently because some students had complained about your use of profanity, and that you once used voodoo-dolls as part of a teaching demonstration, and that you once imitated the bark of a rabid dog so well that several students ran from the room straight to the registrar where they dropped your course, while others complained that your class was "too entertaining." I hope you find all these complaints as silly as I do. I wish Gabriella and I could testify on your behalf!

But was there really some "domestic incident" the cops were called for that resulted in your being arrested at your house by one of your former students? Did you really spend a night in jail? Apparently these things made the local paper, including the online version which prompted many immature comments. Even more malicious gossip was spread over the internet, but I never knew about it (Bill canceled our subscription long ago, thankfully, and I don't go online unless I'm searching for recipes). Regardless, I refuse to cast judgment on any of these things until I hear your point of view because I agree with you when you say "There are always *at least* two sides to every story" (Episode 8).

I'm imploring you now, Dom, to employ the rope-a-dope. You should face the mirror and sing "I'm Still Standing!" You should catch your breath between rounds and talk to someone who understands these things before you throw in the towel. That person is me, Dom. You'd be surprised how well I know you. One thing you should *not* do is beat yourself up. You're a good person, Dom. Sue said you were the first person to greet her when she started there. She said you once helped her move a filing cabinet up four floors to her office because you didn't believe in bothering the poorly paid custodians and because *not* to help would mean that you would just have to go to class, which she thought was funny. She also said you apologized to her for the extra work she'd have while she helped her boss find people to cover your classes. She said you told her to take whatever books she wanted from your office and to donate the rest to the library. She said you left her with a personal check and wrote down a couple of students' names and asked her to see about setting up scholarships (to be anonymous) for those students. Then she said you thanked her for all she'd ever done, and you said goodbye and walked away, looking sadder than she'd ever seen you, which breaks my heart to pieces.

I'm leaving my phone number at the bottom of this letter, Dom. And don't forget: if you need a pick-me-up, Gabriella's birthday party is just a couple days away. I haven't shared any of these details with her. They are irrelevant to what you have meant to her. Please take care of yourself. Please know that we care about you!

Very sincerely yours,
S. (812) 555-2133

11 October

Dear Dom,

This will be my last letter. I suppose you won't get it either, but it makes sense for me to write it. I drove to your apartment today (I admit it's not *exactly* on my route to the grocery store). I summoned enough courage to walk up the stairs and knock on your door, but I saw no signs of life. I wasn't sure what I would say if you had answered, but I knew I wouldn't be able to live with myself if I didn't try to reach out to you.

You missed a good party. My eggplant parmesan was a little off because I had trouble finding non-bruised eggplant and I had trouble concentrating, but Mom and Gabriella said it was fine. Gabriella asked why you hadn't come. I told her you'd written a nice note of regret and that you explained that you had had to fly off to Italy to be with Rosa, your wife. I'm not sorry for lying about this. She got very excited, so happy to learn that two of her favorite people could be happily married and live together in a beautiful place, happily ever after, etc. And right after that, she got fully dressed, she brushed her hair, she put on her good shoes, and she skipped out to the mailbox. At that point, I think she didn't even think of carrying your voice with her, and I was glad.

She found two pieces of mail—one thing was a postcard from Rosa, who had remembered her birthday. The front of the card featured a beautiful photograph of the Teatro alla Scala Opera House in Milan, and on the back Rosa's note said, "Gabriella— you are a smart, talented, beautiful, and amazing woman, and <u>you will go far!</u>" The other thing was the last letter I'd written to you, marked "return to sender," but I don't think she could tell who the letter had been intended for.

I learned about these letters after she came back inside, but just then, it was wonderful for Mom and me to watch her from the window, being so brave and looking so independent. She looked down the street, then up to the clear blue sky and down the street again like she was planning a trip. She looked back at us and smiled the biggest smile I've seen from her in years, and she waved her entire arm as if to say, "Take a good long look because pretty soon I'll be waving from a place where you can't see me!"

I believe her. I wish, on your darkest day, that you could find some comfort in knowing that you (*and* Rosa) helped someone so much. Shouldn't that be enough, Dom? Why couldn't something so rare and precious as that be enough? And wouldn't it help you to know that your DVD classes are available in the public library to help other people—for free? I would call that a successful life, Dom. Why would you call it anything else?

I picture a day in the not-so-distant future when my mother and me will be gone and Gabriella will be alone, playing her piccolo, and I picture you somehow crossing the path of her music and I imagine that moment as a time when both of your hearts will move in sync because of what you gave her that she would right that second be returning to you. I've decided to put down my pen and devote the rest of my good days to try and paint what that moment looks like. Maybe Gabriella will one day hang it on a wall next to Rosa's "Habitat." And maybe she'll tell the story of how those pieces of art came to keep each other company. I hope she'll find someone who needs to hear it as much as she'll need to tell it.

S.

What to Do When Your Spouse Is Burning

Don't talk.

If you make the mistake of talking, don't say, "Well, this is typical."

Don't say, "Can you relax long enough for me to create a cost-benefit-analysis spreadsheet on various resolution strategies that will ensure our highest rate of success in the most efficient manner?"

Don't say, "Hell. Where did I put that thing—the red thing that was lying on the floor of the utility closet for so long it had spider webs all over it and kept getting in the way of my slippers, the—what do you call it—red container-thing with the pull-pin thing on top that you pull out and spray that I tested on the hydrangeas fourteen years ago when I set them on fire, so heroically determined was I to have properly working equipment for such a time as this, though I've admitted it was foolish to burn the hydrangeas. I've apologized a hundred times for that. I'm big enough to say I was wrong on that one. But is the red thing in the garage? Next to the smoke detectors?"

Don't waste time, at *this* time, constructing a time-consuming apology.

Do not say, "I'm sorry I've been such an incendiary device lately. I truly am."

If you make the mistake of constructing an apology while your spouse is burning, do not water it down by attaching excuses. Do not introduce language that deflects blame.

Don't say, "It's not *my* fault." Don't say, "I never learned the basics of fire prevention or fire suppression because my parental models ran for the hills and left me in fire-retardant pajamas that I stopped wearing when we got engaged."

Do not say, "I was too busy for the fifteen years we lived next door to Tim-the-firefighter/EMT to ask his advice on how best to help a spouse should s/he spontaneously combust. I fully intended to invite him over to build a bonfire out back, at which point I planned to hand him a beer and become best friends, quite a plausible plan had I had time to execute it."

Don't say, "I disagree that I have trouble making or keeping friends. I planned to prove this once Tim and I built our bonfire and drank a beer and stared into it while I interviewed him on the fire-safety tips he shared with third-graders, although, honestly, one has to wonder whether Tim would even be a good best friend or whether he would offer credible advice because we know his wife was having an affair with the distilled-water delivery man AND his own house caught fire seven summers ago from a clogged dryer vent (a hazard I inspected every Sunday morning on our own dryer, by the way, though I was too big to brag about it). And when the black smoke poured out of his bottom windows and you said 'DO SOMETHING,' my first thought was to call his cellphone, but then I reflected upon all the reasons (while you dialed 911) that I'd never had a chance to trade numbers with him the way a good neighbor would. I never saw him. If I wasn't in my basement revising the blueprints for my time machine and if he wasn't working at the fire station, he was up early and out late nailing fire-resistant shingles to all of his friends' roofs, or installing high-efficiency insulation at his mother's house, or he was visiting third grade classrooms, and I was pretty busy myself, revising my blueprints, which yes, I agree has taken too long, but you can't imagine the pace at which time-machine technology continues to evolve, the details of which I stopped sharing when you stopped showing interest in my work fourteen years and nine months ago. I also washed the dishes. Cooked a meatloaf (without onions). Hired a horticulturalist so I'd have more time for my time machine. Made the bed. Vacuumed. Very happy, mind you, to do those things for you/us, while you worked that soul-deadening job so I'd have time to stay in the basement, very happy indeed, complaining only moderately I'd say, though I agree it was too much, way too much, and not at all in proportion with the amount of complaint-worthy shit you suffered for sixty-plus hours a week as the paralegal among those blind justice workers at the firm of good ol' boy and boy, though one time, feeling so tender about your wasting your talents there that I was moved to tears, I dropped my pencil and rushed upstairs to say, I'm sorry. I'm sorry you have to work at that place; very soon I'll take us away from here. To which you replied, 'It burns my ass that you use the phrase *have to*.' Which *was* the wrong way to put what I meant to say, I see now, then tried to think of a better way, but you were already smoldering, so I retreated to the basement and made this mental note: 'Make a physical note to look for the red thing with the pull-pin thing.'"

Do not say, "Shoo-wee."

Do not invoke your spouse's family and the potential role you think they *may* have played in making this event inevitable. Do not say, "You know, your father says your great grandfather was pretty hot-tempered."

Do not—though you may now begin to see the severity of the situation and your role in creating conditions that have made it worse—offer your spouse a hug. Take a long step forward and hold the honest and painfully gruesome expression that betrays the stomach-wrenching sadness of the moment and the devastating loneliness it portends. Extend your arms. Then think this: is trying to save someone on fire like trying to save someone who's drowning? Doesn't one need to be sufficiently equipped and properly trained to prevent doubling the number of potential fatalities?

Do not say, "Can we plant rutabaga in our winter garden?"

Postpone the self-loathing that will come from having failed your spouse, and *learn something* from Tim, the quick-thinking, kind-hearted neighbor who will, just that second, jump the fence and rush to your spouse's aid. Tim will take the lead-position in the deft-footed drop and roll he learned in third grade, then offer a freshly distilled bottled water, an ear, a towel, a vodka tonic, a sincere note of empathy, complete agreement on the sorrowful state of the world and the trouble we have living in it which creates such constantly flammable conditions. "I've been burned too," Tim will say. "Not much fun being burned. It's a wonder we're not all burning all the time." Tim will offer to take your spouse swimming at a secluded spot he happens to know, available to heroes. First, he'll insist on rest. He'll say, "I'll pick you up when you recover," giving your spouse something to dream about. Then Tim will pull a guitar from his anus and strum while singing this: "I'm sorry I cannot offer you a hug; it would only cause you pain."

While obsessing over this comparative view of yourself as a slow-thinking, cold-hearted, selfish failure of a spouse, refrain from playing, for hours on end, with endless boxes of matches.

Seclude yourself and listen to your spouse's ghost. The ghost will say, "For fuck's sake. Grow up and stop playing with matches. It's a pitiful self-pitying and pathetic ploy to cast yourself as a victim you hope someone will think worth dowsing. Force yourself to face a mirror."

Face a mirror.

Shake your head. Say, "Good golly, miss molly."

Respect the mess you've made.

Forgive the fire; it is innocent.

Become best friends with Viktor E. Frankl.

Take time to shred those silly time-machine blueprints you've wasted your life on.

Study the nervous system of the fruit fly. Study its aggression gene. There are many genes that play a furtive role, especially in males who compete for the attention of females.

Listen to your spouse's ghost long after you've grown deaf. This won't be difficult.

Listen to the ghost while you lose your hair, your muscle mass, your balance, your sense of smell, your teeth, your taste, your sight, your hippocampus.

Stare at the ashes inside the urn you hope she would have liked and say good night, say good morning, say good afternoon, say good night.

Say, "Fine. I will turn my new work toward forgiving myself for giving you the final word."

The Funeral Starts at Two

We were neck-deep, my father-in-law and me, holding to the concrete edge of the saltwater swimming pool he'd installed last spring (at the age of seventy-seven, to the great shock of everyone), eye-level with the dead grass that went as far as the woods, which went as deep as the eye could see. We were talking. Or rather, *he* was talking and I was listening, which was fine with me. His brother's funeral was two hours away, so he had important things on his mind. He had things that needed saying.

He said, "I'm not going."

It was late July, and the water was already too warm. It hadn't rained in seven weeks, and the dark cloud behind us didn't tease him into thinking the drought would end today. On the patio, his radio's antennae stretched toward Nashville's WSM, 650 AM, where Hank Williams now sang of crying moons and weeping robins and lonely whippoorwills.

"I don't think I could survive it," he said. "It would make me remember too many sad and crazy things I'd rather not remember."

I liked to watch his eyes. Tiny sparks still burned in them, like fires in a cave. He'd lived a long time with the habit of noticing things, and despite everything he already knew so well (like the woods we looked into now), he kept looking for something

new. Just now, I imagined him staring into the woods at Hank
Williams, who was leaning against a tree in his white suit and
white boots, holding his hat over his heart, staring at a lovesick
whippoorwill.

He said, "Me and my brother went to *Hank's* funeral. I didn't
want to go—I couldn't afford to take a day off—but he *begged* me
to go with him, maybe because we'd met Hank that one time, so I
took a day off and went, rode there with Dale Gillis, this old boy
worked with us at the plant, poor guy dropped dead from a heart
attack on the loading dock when he was forty years old, left three
little kids. Hank died on the first day of 1953, twenty-nine years
old. We were nineteen. Dale Gillis was thirty-five at the time, and
he cried all the way there and all the way back, drove off the road
three times and like to killed us claiming he couldn't see for crying, and he told us then too, said his wife had been two-timing
him, good ol' boy from Montgomery, same place Hank and Lillie,
his mother, moved to when Hank was a kid. She ran a boarding
house there, cooked some meals for Tee-Tot, this street-musician
who taught Hank how to play some blues-guitar, probably taught
Hank how to drink too, I don't know, but Montgomery is where
Hank saw the light one night coming back from being on the
road a long time—they always had trouble waking him up because
he'd be passed out in the back of his Cadillac, which is where
his driver, man name of Charles Carr, found him dead while they
were headed to some shows in Ohio and West Virginia, no telling how long he'd been dead, some claim he'd gotten a morphine
injection on account of his bad back and maybe had too much
booze to go with it, I don't know, but Charles couldn't shake him
awake that time. Normally if they were coming home, he'd shake
him awake while they still had a few miles to go, give him time
to get himself together so he wouldn't look *too* drunk when Lillie
saw him, that woman was half-mean, but she'd had a hard time of
it, her husband took sick and stayed in the hospital eight or nine

years while Hank was growing up, and their first house burned down and she had a son die on her soon after he was born, but close to Montgomery there one night they shook him awake and first thing he saw was that light, must've been the water-tower light, but he saw the light and knew he was almost home, so he said 'Praise the Lord' then he wrote that song in the backseat before he got home, made it a gospel song, which wasn't hard for him to do, Lillie was a fierce Christian woman, always made him go to church while he was growing up, stayed after him to do right, and maybe he felt guilty for drinking so much all the time too, I don't know. But my brother and me met him in the fall of 1949, after he'd come to Nashville in the *spring* of '49—Lillie and Audrey, his wife—she was a mean woman too, but he loved her something awful, she's the one give him the lovesick blues—they pushed him to leave home and make some money. He'd always been lazy and didn't care much about traveling, but one day in October, he stepped into WSM where me and my brother were standing with our Future Farmers of America group just after we'd finished reading a little script for part of the Noontime Neighbors show they did, guy name of John McDonald hosted it every day for twenty-seven years until they took him off the air in 1972, but just after he finished giving the farm news is when Hank came strolling in with his guitar and stopped and shook our hands. It was a Friday. He was in town for the Friday Night Frolic, WSM's radio show that was a warm up to Saturday night's Opry, a lot of the singers would stop in after Noontime Neighbors, so that's how we got to see him sing 'Lovesick Blues' and 'My Bucket's Got a Hole In It,' and three years later, we drove to his funeral, got in a mile-long line just to walk by his casket. He claimed in one of his songs that he'd have to hire somebody to cry for him at his funeral, figured nobody would be lonely for him, but he was wrong—poor old Dale Gillis had the worse-sobbing fit of any grown man I've ever seen, then at Dale's funeral of course they had to play a couple of Hank's songs, which must've made Dale happy because everybody there was boo-hooing like crazy, including me and my brother, I never will forget."

He squinted toward the woods as if Hank was looking back at him, winking, while his voice magically came behind us, singing . . . *like me, he's lost the will to live, I'm so lonesome, I—*

"I can't go," he said. "Even if it *is* just across town, remember yesterday where I was showing you all around Culleoka and that cemetery where all my people are, my little son, and everybody over on that hill next to Uncle Hillary's old house, where he slept on the roof like I told you about—that's where the funeral is."

I said I remembered, but there had been a lot to see, and volumes of exquisitely detailed commentary to go with it, most of which I'd already forgotten.

I said, "Let's get ready. I'll drive." I didn't understand how he couldn't attend his own brother's funeral. He had nothing bad to say about him. I thought of my own brother, a banker in Charlotte whom I didn't even like and rarely talked to and would never miss, but I knew I'd go to his funeral if he should croak, only to observe the custom and be a comfort to my parents, who *did* like him (for reasons unknown to me). And wouldn't the funeral force me to forgive our differences and make me think harder about being more alive and less selfish? Isn't that what funerals were good for? Wasn't it sacrilegious *not* to go?

He said, "What time is it?"

I looked at my phone, which I'd placed on the concrete in front of me so I could answer when his daughter called to check our progress. We'd agreed earlier that morning that I would drive him to the church, and she and her mother would meet us there early enough for my wife and me to change into the clothes she was out buying for us. We hadn't packed for a funeral. Three days ago, we'd driven eight hundred miles from Wisconsin (where jobs had taken us) for a brief visit, to see the pool—so expensive and out of character that we said we wouldn't believe it until we'd gotten wet. His brother, whom my wife hadn't seen in twenty years, died on our way. My father-in-law didn't go to the visitation, claiming he wasn't in the mood for the kind of party those things turned into, and he didn't want to go to the funeral either, but he had said he would. I wanted to take him. I wanted to sit inside an old country church and consume all the sorrow and music the occasion made available, to hear the eulogies and the stories afterward and to be reminded, as poetically as possible, of the certain death we were all speeding toward.

"It's 12:30." I stared at him as if to suggest he should move toward the shower.

He grimaced. His eyes got smaller. I imagined him wondering who had planned a funeral for the hottest part of the day when he'd have to sweat in a hot suit inside a hot church and stand in the hellish graveside-heat at the height of the hottest summer he'd known in a long history of hot summers he'd finally counterpunched, in part, by paying a small fortune for a pool he'd enjoy for a few summers only, at best.

After the commercials that followed Hank, Patsy Cline said, *Crazy.*

He said, "You ought to know what kind of family you've married into." He laughed at this, then turned somber. "But I don't feel up to rehashing any of those old stories about that crazy bunch right now, be honest with you. Not even Uncle Perry, who sat on duck eggs. Or Uncle Hillary, who slept on the roof. Or Uncle Joe who went crazy from grief and nearly got me and my brother killed one time in a—reckon you better answer that?"

I answered my ringing phone.

My wife said, "You'll have to help him put on his socks. Is he getting ready?"

"No."

"Speed him up. Is he in the *pool?*"

"Yes."

"Oh, good Christ. I'm in the mall, and I can't find a dress. I've also lost my mother." Then she hung up.

He said, "You ever know anybody go crazy from grief? Happens all the time, I reckon, but Uncle Joe, he ran over his own son in his own streetcar he was driving in Nashville. His boy run right out in front of him and waved to get his Daddy's attention, then Joe looked into his eyes and run right over him, nothing he could do. But he was crazy before that. Mama said he was a high-tempered man when she met him, said there was something peculiar about him made her nervous. You never went to their house when there wasn't a loaded gun in every corner. This was long about the time of Dillinger and Bonnie and Clyde and them, and that made Mama nervous too because Joe liked those folks too much, which was bad, after they'd killed all those people. Anyway, one Friday evening we went out to stay with him and Aunt Maude, and I could tell he was already in a foul mood, acted like we were bothering him just to be there. Next morning, he started showing me and my brother all his chickens—this was just a year or so after he'd run over his son—but I remember him walking through the yard—"

My phone dinged from a text. *are you in the pool too?* I didn't answer.

"—but every time he saw a weak chicken, he'd reach down and pull its head off without breaking stride. They weren't going to survive anyway, those weak ones, but it upset me walking along behind him, I had to be careful not to step on the chicken heads he was throwing down with all the headless chickens dancing around our legs. I don't think it bothered my brother as much as it did me—he just kind of laughed it off. But Uncle Joe he did that for a little while, and then he stopped there in the yard and looked at me like he wanted to pull *my* head off."

He paused because a long peal of thunder had unrolled itself. When he looked at me, I pointed over my right shoulder, where the sky was still blue. Ten years ago, a virus left him deaf in his right ear and made it hard for him to locate the directions of certain sounds.

Patsy gave way to Eddy Arnold, who sang "Make the World Go Away."

"The *Tennessee Plowboy*," my father-in-law said. "Born right over here just this side of Henderson, died a few years ago. Daddy was a sharecropper."

I said, "Maybe we should get out of the water."

He looked toward his neighbor's house. "Opal ought to come running across the yard any second, poor thing. Usually, she's on my couch before the first crack of thunder's over with, she's so bad to get scared in a storm, been running over here for forty years, even when her husband was alive, which I always thought was strange, but I never said anything. She must've felt safer over here for some reason, which is fine—she don't hurt nobody. But Uncle Joe, he looked at me real hard and he told me, said 'go get your Aunt Maude, tell her we're going to town.' So we all piled up in his car— he had this A-Model Ford, nice car, had the side-platform on it like Bonnie and Clyde's car. Time we got a mile down the road, Aunt Maude asked him, said 'Just where are we headed?' and he said, plain as day, said, 'I'm fixin' to kill Dr. Drew and then I'm going to kill my brother Ernest.' Dr. Drew was the doctor treated their other child that got sick and died about six months after their first child died. I reckon Joe thought Dr. Drew hadn't done enough to help the child, I don't know. And Uncle Ernest, he was the one talked Daddy into buying his farm and talked Joe into buying his—he was the oldest kid in that bunch of thirteen kids, and he was always trying to run everybody else's life, always pushing people into making bad decisions. Anyway, Joe, he sped on—"

Another text: *mom says to put him in his tan suit.*

"—and finally stopped at Dr. Drew's house, got out and opened the trunk and pulled out two handguns and walked up the porch steps and banged on his door, and when Dr. Drew opened it, Joe lifted his gun and went to shoot him right between the eyes, but Dr. Drew ducked just enough for the bullet to part his hair. I remember Dr. Drew. I remember the scar he had right up through there, which he had to answer for the rest of his life—then he slammed the door and run got in the fireplace, him and his wife both squatted down in the fireplace while Joe went around to all the windows and kept on shooting. Back then, they had a constable name of Seth Young, and somebody called him, and I guess somebody called the sheriff too, but it would've taken the sheriff an hour to show up, so Seth Young and some of his crew went down there, tried to get Joe to stop shooting, but then Joe started shooting at them while he was walking back toward the car where we was all crouched down—at least *I* was crouched down—I was curled up under the seat far as I could go, but my brother, he was sitting up watching the whole thing play out, and Aunt Maude, poor thing, she was—"

He stopped when it thundered again and looked at me. I pointed over my head to exaggerate the closeness. I said, "Let's surrender. Head for dry ground." He looked past me toward Opal's empty yard and pinched his lower lip like he did when something worried him.

"Aunt Maude screamed for Joe to throw down his gun and give up, but he kept shooting while he walked back to the car, calm-as-you-please, and finally, he opened his door and got half-way in and started shooting out the *passenger* side window, right across Aunt Maude. Mama said she saw the coat Aunt Maude was wearing—tall fur all-round the neck, pretty fancy for the time—Mama said there were powder burns all over that fur. But they kept shooting it out until somebody finally hit him. I never saw it, I was still up under the seat covering my head, but my brother claimed he saw Chapman, the blacksmith, hiding behind a tree—claimed he was the one who finally shot and killed him."

He pinched his bottom lip and squinted toward the woods as if Joe and Maude were standing shoulder-to-shoulder beside Hank, posing for a picture in their Sunday best, Joe in a suit with a vest and top hat, Maude in her powder-burned coat, each with a palm on the head of a pale child, all their faces devoid of smiles.

Eddy Arnold gave way to Jim Reeves, who said, "There's a blizzard coming on."

"Gentleman Jim Reeves," he said. "Died in the little plane he was flying into Nashville in 1964, right around this time of year, flew straight into a thunderstorm up here in Brentwood, forty years old, killed him and his manager both."

The song made it clear that the blizzard was going to kill him too—him *and* his horse, before they made it home to Mary Ann. It was a tearjerker.

Last night, a wild-animal scream woke my wife and me at two a.m. It was louder and more primitive than anything we'd ever heard. Her first thought was that her father's cherished cat—what had once been a wild and starving tom he'd rescued and tamed enough to take to the vet for shots—had lost a fight with one of the bobcats some people claimed were roaming around killing people's calves and goats and puppies. When we ran into the moon-lit yard, we saw no animals, but we both heard a large creature scampering off through the woods. When we mentioned the animal-scream to her father at breakfast, he showed no concern, said his cat would show up for lunch.

He said, "Patsy Cline died in a plane crash the year before Jim Reeves did, got into some bad fog and crashed in a forest sixty miles from here, little town called Fatty Bottom. Her pilot and Jim Reeves both were trained by the same man, apparently. She was thirty years old. Just before that, she'd started giving away all her things, claimed she knew she was about to die. That feeling must've hit her in 1961, about the time she had a head-on collision on Old Hickory Boulevard. She hit the windshield, busted her head open, nearly died right there. I've always hated driving around Nashville—you've never seen so many blind people in a rush. Be careful driving back through there on your way home, I'd take the bypass if I was you, but not at rush hour. The day after Patsy had that wreck is when Bobby Deal, Nutty Deal's brother— these boys I grew up with who had a little farm down next to ours, we used to play together all the time whenever we could, and Bobby, he was a little-off—he wasn't as nutty as Nutty was— but Bobby, he come to the plant next morning singing 'I Fall to Pieces,' and he kept singing it all day *long*, which got kindly tiresome by four o'clock in the evening. But I remember that because ten years later, I had to fire him from the plant, and a year after that, he shot himself in the head right in front of his wife and kids. Me and my brother had a chance to stop him, and maybe we could have, I don't know."

It thundered again, and again he looked at me, and again I pointed straight above. I said, "Let's retreat."

"I always liked Bobby alright, even though they was something in his sense of humor that scared me a little bit, but he'd had some hard times growing up just like we did, and he never really bothered nobody, and he was a deacon in our church too, so we all just kind of left him alone. But then I got promoted to supervisor and became his *boss*, which he resented, since we'd grown up together and went through all the same hard times, but the last time I saw him, just before he shot himself, I was driving through town with my brother—"

My phone dinged again, but I didn't look.

"—we saw him pull up next to us at a red light down across from where the Walmart is now, which was a hayfield then, owned by Billy Brock who trained Tennessee walking horses, mistreated them something awful, *soring* their front legs with chains and chemicals so they'd lift them higher than all those other hurt walking horses that competed every year over in

Shelbyville—there was a big write-up about it in the *Tennessean* here a while back, made me sick to my stomach to read what-all they did to those horses, but Bobby, I hated to fire him—"

I looked at my phone for my wife's text: *mom says let him pick out his own tie.*

"—he needed that job. There weren't no other jobs around here, but I was the shift supervisor and he pulled that beer out of his lunchbox right there in the cafeteria in front of forty other guys after I'd already told him two other times not to bring beer to work, so I didn't have much of a choice—he was operating dangerous machinery and *my* bosses stayed on me about safety, we'd already had guys losing fingers and parts of arms and this one ol' boy, Ben Pierce from over this side of Pulaski, he fell off some scaffolding one day, paralyzed himself from the neck down, and then his wife left him alone with their two little kids after that, poor guy. But a year after I fired Bobby, he stopped there at that red light and shouted through his window at us, said 'Y'all come have a cup of coffee with me.' I told him we had to get to the ballpark—we played on a softball team together, I played second base and my brother played shortstop and he hated to lose a ballgame more than anybody I've ever known, that rascal *hated* to lose, whether it was cards, marbles, checkers, horseshoes, he'd cheat to keep from losing, we both got our tempers from Daddy, but his was worse than mine, you've never seen a grown man throw the kind of fit he would for losing. So I told Bobby, said we'd better take a rain check, and he winked at me and waved and the light turned green and we drove on. Next day, I learned he'd shot himself. Sat on the couch between his children and put a gun in his mouth and pulled the trigger. He crosses my mind just about every day, but I wish he'd stop it."

He squinted toward the woods as if Bobby Deal were stepping forward with a coffee cup in one hand and a gun in the other, smiling to show the hole that went through the back of his mouth and out the back of his head, singing "I Fall to Pieces" along with Patsy Cline, who stood next to him, her bleeding head on the shoulder of Gentleman Jim Reeves.

He said, "What time is it?"

"Five after one. We'd better get going."

It thundered again, and again he looked at me, and again I pointed straight above my head. I said, "Let's go."

"If it comes from the east, you better watch out, but that little cloud back there, it'll move around us sure as hell. That's what Daddy said every time he spotted a raincloud and we'd need it to rain so bad. He'd look at me and my brother and he'd say, 'It'll move around us sure as hell.' And then it would. He'd stand outside and watch it slide around us until it stopped over our neighbor's farm and started raining. Then he'd go to cussing. If it didn't rain, we didn't eat. But if it ever did come a little rain, like late at night while everybody else was sleeping hard after working all day in the fields, he'd still be half-awake, half-hoping to hear a little rain hit the tin roof and half-afraid a storm was going to blow the crops away—I'm not sure he got a full night's sleep in forty years—but if he ever heard a little rain hit the roof, he'd jump out the bed and run outside completely naked—he slept without any clothes on in the summertime because it stayed so hot inside that house, we never did have air conditioning, even after we signed up for electricity in 1950, which is about the time you got it if you lived back in the hills like we did—we had to drive up to Shelbyville to sign up for it with Duck River Electric, then they come out and put up the poles and run the lines, but we never did have air conditioning. We got a icebox and an electric stove and thought we was uptown because we didn't have to chop stove wood any more, but we still chopped enough to heat the house, and Mama got her a ringer-washing machine, had to run a hose from the sink through the living room window out to the porch where she kept it. Better answer your phone."

I answered. My wife said, "What color are the walls in our bedroom?"

"The walls in our bedroom?"

"What color are they?"

"Brown?"

"No, they are most certainly not *brown*. They have some deals on curtains here, but I can't remember what color our walls are. Is he ready yet?"

"No."

"Get a move on." Then she hung up.

He said, "They put in the bathroom in 1955, and we got a water heater, got a pump put in down by the spring that carried water to the house, but when it rained at night, Daddy, he'd run outside buck-naked and stand there with his arms spread wide and his face turned up. He'd stay out there until it quit raining because he thought it was bad luck to walk back out of it again." He laughed at this, a hard chuckle that came up from his abdomen, which I always liked to see. Then he squinted toward the woods again, as if his naked father were out there staring toward the cloud, begging for it to come wash over him. He said, "I can't go to that funeral."

The cloud moved closer and darkened a patch of sky. He looked toward Opal's yard.

He said, "What time is it?"

"Time to get out of the water."

"Yeah," he said. "We'd better get out of the water." He pushed off from the wall and started toward the shallow end, moving his head from side to side, leaving me behind.

We dried off with the towels we'd left out. Then he sat and stared toward his neighbor's yard. He said, "If Opal don't come running soon, we may have to go check on her."

I put my phone on top of the newspapers we'd left on the patio table and turned down the endless radio commercials and promotions. The patio had a porch overhang, and above the table, a ceiling fan stayed on low to keep flies away. This is where we read three morning newspapers over breakfast and coffee, lingering over the strange and sordid stories that gave us solace because we could shake our heads at the wickedness in the world, such as the local story we'd read this morning of a thirteen-year-old girl who knocked on a preacher's door and asked for a Bible lesson, then stabbed him thirty-three times. It's where we ate a light lunch, it's where we ate dinner, it's where we watched the sun rise and sink while we faced the woods and let time unroll itself through the quiet days of a Tennessee summer, without protest. Sometimes, I'd go for a thirty-minute run through surrounding subdivisions and return to cool off in the pool and warm up again in the sun and dread the inevitable trip back, which would mean I'd have to face, too soon, an inhospitable Wisconsin winter that could last five months.

He said, "Bitty-kitty better get his butt home." He pinched his lip and looked to his left for his cat and to his right for Opal.

He said, "What time is it?"

"One-fifteen. Let's go."

"Thunder never bothered Mrs. Davis. 'Course she was stone-deaf, so that helped." His neighbor on the other side, a ninety-year-old widow he'd always called *Mrs.* Davis, died three months ago. Her empty house worried him. He missed knowing she was there, as she had been for fifty years, and he worried over the changes new neighbors might bring.

"But she'd call me every time she saw a spider, and I'd run over and save the day. Poor *Mr.* Davis, he's still spinning in his grave after her funeral—I know I told you about their son showing up with his new wife."

The sixty-five-year-old Davis son—a twice-married man with four children whose father had instilled the traditional obsession of guns, football, and Civil War history, had caused a scandal by marrying a transgendered woman he brought to his mother's funeral. My father-in-law had been genuinely pleased, while telling this story, that there was still something in the world that could surprise him. He said he'd congratulated the newly-weds and invited them to go swimming in his new pool, an invitation the trans partner accepted at ten o'clock the night of the funeral, saying she'd like to relax and get her mind off death. My father-in-law brought her a towel, told her to stay as long as she wanted, sincerely happy that his pool could be of use.

"I didn't like going to that funeral either," he said. "But I went." He squinted toward the woods, as if Mrs. Davis was standing out there waving with a white-gloved hand, casting a disapproving glance toward Hank, who pulled a flask from his back pocket.

"I can't go to this one." He stared toward the woods as if there were rows of wooden pews out there filled with people sobbing.

I pointed to the far side of his carport, where he kept a bowl full of cat food, which just now, a raccoon was eating from. She sat on her hind legs and looked around. When it thundered again, she rushed to scoop food to her mouth, alternating both hands, hurrying to eat and run before the storm broke open.

He said, "That's the funniest thing I've ever seen. I hate to see anything go hungry. You hungry? I'm not too hungry, but I reckon I could eat a little bite. That's what Uncle Perry used to say, then he'd eat for about three hours straight and clean us out. If you go in there and bring us back a couple left-over biscuits with a piece of that country ham, I'll tell you about Uncle Perry."

When I went to the kitchen and pulled a small plate from the cabinet, a rusty voice said "*Hey!*" and scared me so badly I jumped and yelled like a little girl and looked into the bad light of the living room where an old lady sat on the couch, rocking, staring back at me. She had tall and wild grey hair, and she was wearing a white robe.

I said, "You okay, Opal?"

"They's a bad storm coming. Y'all better get out that water."

I didn't know if I needed to tell her that I was already out of the water. I said, "We'll be right out here if you need us."

She said, "I don't know where in the world I'd go if they weren't here, do you?" She didn't wait for me to answer. She turned her head away and kept rocking.

I took the biscuits outside, told my father-in-law that Opal was on his couch, and he nodded, seeming relieved that she was safe.

He said, "Opal grew up rougher than we did over there other side of Lynnville, her folks had a little farm and struggled all their lives, and I reckon they went through some bad storms too, worse one we had was the 1948 tornado took the roof off our house and blew our barn down while Daddy and my brother and me were inside of it. It was a Saturday. Daddy saw the storm coming, so he climbed to the top of the barn and tried to get down whatever tobacco he could, and about the time he heard it bearing down on him, he yelled at my brother and me, said run lay in the ditch, so we did—we run out there and lay side by side in the ditch and watched things fly over our heads—jars of fruit, boards with nails sticking out—but Daddy, he stayed in the top of the barn trying to get down his tobacco and that tornado got on top of him in a hurry, so he grabbed that pole and held tight and the wind bent that pole all the way over and just kind of laid him on the ground. All the tobacco got scattered all over the hill, but we gathered what we could afterward and brought it back and stripped it. There weren't much left. Funny thing is it didn't *rain* that much. It blew our smokehouse away and all our canned goods with it. But we spent a couple days hunting down all the fruit jars we could—the ones that didn't hit rocks and break, we brought back to the house. We were more worried about the tobacco and the food than we were the house. We nearly starved to death that year. That was in October because we didn't have any meat get blown away, which means we hadn't killed a hog yet. It blew away the garage and the smokehouse and the henhouse—they just disappeared. Flattened our barn and blew the roof off our house—picked up the roof and carried it off while Mama was inside the house. We had a log room that was the original house, just a one-room log house like a lot a-people had, and we'd built on to it over the years, but she ran into that log room, where she crouched down and watched the roof fly off. It messed up the rest of house too, but we were more worried about the barn. We *had* to have a barn. So we slept without a roof for a few days. I'd lay in bed and look up at the stars, which was peaceful. Then finally that next weekend, some of the neighbors who didn't get any damage, they come and helped us—Bobby and Nutty Deal and their folks, they helped us gather up all the tin that blew all over the hillside, and we brought it back down and straightened it out best we could and nailed it back on the house. Didn't have a nickel's worth of insurance. We had some timber, and we tried to cut the timber to rebuild the barn—old poplar trees about fifty feet tall, but we didn't know what we were doing, ended up splitting the trees, and finally had to go to the sawmill and ask them to come cut them down for us, and they came out—that was the first chainsaw I'd ever seen—they had a two-man chainsaw you could hear from ten miles off, drove all the rattlesnakes away from there for a year or two. Brought their own mules to drag the timber down the hill. What time is it?"

"One twenty-five. If you get dressed now, we can make it."

"We nearly starved to death that year. Mama had a hard time keeping us fed, and they was some nights—you ever tried to go to sleep with a empty stomach? It's hard to do. And Uncle Perry, he'd usually show up around dinner time. Mama hated to see him coming—he could eat more than any man I've ever seen. She didn't have the heart to turn him away, and Daddy, he'd say, 'better come have a bite with us, Perry,' and Perry'd say, 'I ain't hungry, but I reckon I could eat a little bite,' then he'd sit down and

clean us out. While he was cleaning *us* out, his mare was cleaning our barn out—he had this little ol' mare he called Mary, and
he always left her in our barn so she could eat up all our hay
and corn—we could barely keep our own animals from starving.
But Perry never bothered nobody, even when he was sitting on
his duck eggs. He'd have a little spell ever once in a while where
he felt like he needed to sit on some duck eggs. Carried them
around in his pockets, and sometimes he'd just get a notion to
stack them in the corner of a room and squat over them—he
didn't really *sit* on them, because of course they'd break, but he'd
squat over them for a good long while and we'd just leave him
alone. None of 'em ever hatched that I know of. Last time we
saw him, he showed up one summer day on Mary—I felt sorry
for her because Perry weighed three hundred pounds, and he
showed up that day strapped down with two hundred pounds'
worth of log chains wrapped around him, *heavy* chains, and he
was holding a shotgun across his lap, and he told us, said he'd
decided to go west and be a cowboy. Then he took off across
the hill, headed east. The way he went across those hills, I knew
from watching him over the years that he liked to avoid the
roads, so he'd cut across those hills, and every time he got to a
fence, he'd get off Mary and lift her over it. He was the stron-
gest man in the county, the blacksmith used to call on him to
carry kegs of horseshoes from the wagon that delivered them
while everybody stood around and watched him and shook their
heads. Daddy was *almost* as strong, but Uncle Perry, he'd lift
Mary's front two legs over the fence, then he'd go around and
lift her back end over the fence and he'd say, 'You carried me
awhile, now I'll carry you.' But he took off that day to be a cowboy, headed east, and that was the last time we saw him."

He squinted toward the darkening woods as if Uncle Perry
was leading Mary through the trees, log chains wrapped around
his chest, carrying a duck egg in the palm of his free hand. It

thundered again, and again he looked at me. I pointed over my right shoulder.

He said, "What time is it?"

"One-thirty. Let's go."

"Maybe Nutty tracked down Uncle Perry. Last time we saw Nutty, that's what he said—said he was lonesome for Uncle Perry so he was going to go find him and bring him home. And maybe he did find him, but I doubt it, 'cause Nutty went west and Perry went east. They used to give Nutty a hard time, poor fella. My brother and Nutty's brother, Bobby, they played this game where they'd take a football and tie it up in a mill sack and then they'd hook the sack to a rope they'd throw over a tree limb. Then they'd string up some barbed wire around some posts to make a boxing ring where that football would be hanging down in the middle of it and two people stood on opposite sides of that football, which was a punching bag. You were supposed to hit the football so it would hit the other guy in the face, but my brother, he'd get Nutty in there standing on the other side of that football and he'd act like—"

He started laughing again and had to stop and start again.

"He'd act like he accidentally missed the football so he could hit Nutty in the nose. And my brother, he'd say, 'Sorry, Nutty,' and Nutty, he'd say, 'Oh that's alright.' Then they'd start up again and my brother would miss the football and pop Nutty's nose again and send the slobber flying and he'd say, 'Sorry, Nutty,' and Nutty'd say, 'That's alright,' and he'd get off the ground again and wipe the blood and snot off his nose and stand there on the other side of that football and raise his fists and my brother would pop him again and apologize again. When my brother got tired of hitting him, Nutty's brother, Bobby, took his place and did the same thing, and poor ol' Nutty—about the time it got dark and they had to quit, his face would be all bloody and his nose would be twisted around to his ear, busted all to pieces, but then we'd lead him around to the side of the house and clean him up good and then take him in the house for dinner and he'd just eat and smile the whole time and compliment Mama's cooking. Last time we saw him, me and my brother were riding together across town for another ballgame, we were in our middle twenties by then, and Nutty was walking along with his thumb out, so we picked him up. That's when he said he was heading off to find Uncle Perry. Didn't have a bag or nothing. I tried to talk him out of it, but he was determined, so I finally let him out and gave him whatever money I had in my pocket—maybe enough to eat on for a couple days, but my brother, he acted like he didn't have any money and looked at me like I was being stupid for giving him *my* money. That was the last time we saw Nutty."

He squinted into the woods toward Nutty, who must've been smiling back at him, blood dripping across his teeth, one arm around Uncle Perry's shoulders. A singer came on I didn't recognize.

I said, "We'd better get going."

"Jimmie Rodgers," he said. "Called him 'The Singing Brakeman' because he worked on the railroad up until he got tuberculosis in his late-twenties. Died when he was about thirty-five. My daddy worked on the railroad too, and I've always wondered why he *quit*. If he'd a-stayed on, it would've spared us some beatings. Would've spared my mama a whole world-of-suffering. But he let Uncle Ernest talk him into buying that sorry piece of land so he could become a dirt farmer and worry himself to death and get meaner every year. Had to work longer days and never knew from one year to the next whether he could hold on to the place. The railroad—it paid him cash *every two weeks*, 35 cents an hour *and* he got a house furnished to him. The railroad wasn't going nowhere—if you had a cause to go somewhere, you rode the train. Everybody had *a local*, a little station they stopped at every few miles where they'd drop off deliveries or pick up milk and stuff for you and take it to town if you had something to sell, and usually wherever that station was would be a section gang, and that section gang took care of seven miles of track—*gandy dancers*, is what they called the section hands, they'd steady be changing out crossties and straightening track. You had to be tough. Uncle Hillary was tough. He was Daddy's section foreman, supervised seven people. Seven people working on seven miles of track, worked the Pan Am line that went from Cincinnati to New Orleans, which Hank sang about, but Jimmie Rodgers he got his start listening to—I know you've heard those old railroad songs where people sing together to stay in rhythm while they hammering on the tracks—that's what Jimmie Rodgers heard growing up that stuck with him so good, but I can't imagine Daddy ever singing." He laughed at this. "They's a picture around here somewhere of Daddy and—"

A new text: *we're driving to the funeral now. You'd better be too. I'm hungry.*

"—beside the tracks and Uncle Hillary with his overalls on and his hands behind his back and his chin lifted up, and my Daddy and four blacks and three whites—back then the blacks and whites around there worked right alongside each other without any problems at all—but in that picture they was all so dirty and sweaty it was hard to tell them apart. It was tough work. Hottest place in the world in the summer. No such thing as shade along a railroad track—and in the winter it was the coldest place because there's nothing to knock the wind off of you. You had to be tough. Daddy had twelve brothers and sisters and they went hungry sometimes too, and my brother, he was tough, but I never was that tough." He stared into the woods, and I looked at the spot where he was staring, as if Jimmie Rodgers was leaning on the other side of the same tree Hank was leaning against, both of them peering toward the darkening sky.

I said, "We need to go now." I spoke more loudly and leaned forward to encourage him.

"Crazy thing is, Daddy ended up having to loan Uncle Hillary money from time to time because he was so bad to gamble. After he got paid, he'd go off on a drinking and gambling spree and come home broke and Aunt Lizzie would try to murder him. Mama took me and my brother down to Lizzie's one morning for something and we were all sitting on the porch and all of a sudden the train stopped at the station right down from us, and we saw this person get off and Mama said, 'that's a strange-looking woman,' because it didn't look like anybody that lived around there, everybody knew everybody else, even all the blacks and whites lived there together right beside the tracks, but here come this strange person marching toward us carrying these flowers high up in the air, and finally Aunt Lizzie, she realized it was Uncle Hillary wearing a dress. Had his work boots on too. He'd bought Aunt Lizzie a new dress or either won it in a crap game, and—"

He started laughing and had to stop, then he tried to talk and had to stop again because he was laughing so hard. It was the kind of laugh I loved seeing from him, rare in anyone, but the kind of laugh that made his mouth open so wide I could see the gap in the rear of his upper row of teeth, where one tooth was missing. I wished then that I could laugh like that. I wished I knew more people who laughed like that. Then he tried to talk while he kept laughing, words spilling out in rocky waves that made me have to listen harder.

"And he kept walking up the tracks and held that bouquet of flowers out ahead of him like it was a olive branch, and she ran out there next to the tracks and scooped up some rocks and started throwing them at his head until he finally threw down those flowers and high-tailed it back the other way in his dress and boots, running and yelling with his arms flailing all around. My brother and me, we laughed about Uncle Hillary and Aunt Lizzie the whole time we were growing up. But sometimes it wasn't funny.

He made it worse for everybody." He squinted toward the woods as if Uncle Hillary and Aunt Lizzie were standing out there in matching dresses, waving, Hillary holding a bouquet of crushed flowers, Lizzie gripping a rock.

The cloud was over us now, and it was darker, but there was no rain.

I stood up. I said, "Let's go."

He said, "My cat better come on home. There's a barn down yonder he likes to go—this barn where this family used to raise rabbits they'd take and sell to Vanderbilt medical school so they could use them for testing—used to take three trucks of rabbits up there every week, I never cared for how they raised them like that just to kill them—but Bitty, he likes to go down there to that barn to do his hunting. He'd better hurry on home. This one's not going to move around us."

And just like that, a few fat drops fell on the patio roof above our heads, and then they dropped around the yard like strewn rocks before it all came bursting down at once in thick sheets of hail. The air around us cooled, and the smell of wet earth blew into the patio and hovered.

He said, "You'd better call them up. Tell them we're not going. Tell them to get on home so they're not driving around in this."

I hadn't worried about them driving until he mentioned it. I'd never been one to get too worried too easily, but suddenly it felt stupid *not* to worry.

It thundered again and grew darker. Down at the highway, a half-mile away, a siren went wailing by. I sat again and reached for my phone and texted this: *not going. come home.*

Someone came on singing "You Win Again," but it wasn't Hank's version, it was Roy Acuff, though I'm not sure how I knew this. My father-in-law, out of character now, refrained from commenting on Roy. He stayed silent and watched the hail come down and let Roy sing.

Any number of bad things could happen. And I remembered that my wife's eyesight wasn't the greatest (though her mother's was worse), and when conditions turned bad, she'd grow more anxious, as if she *expected* something bad to happen, which made her driving worse.

He stared through the rain toward the woods and squinted as if he saw something new. I looked at my phone again, still blank. I watched him watch the hail until the hail gave way to heavy rain. He looked on both sides of him, as if to gauge whether it was lighter in one direction and whether it showed signs of letting up, but it was uniformly heavy and looked to be long-lasting. He pinched his lower lip.

I called my wife. She didn't answer. I feared something bad had already happened. I told myself that she was driving and concentrating, that a ringing phone would make her nervous enough to wreck, so I hung up. I looked out at the rain with my father-in-law. His eyes grew wet and they darted around to different spots. He looked out there and pinched his lower lip, and I did the same, while we waited and worried, silently, together, for a long stretch of time I would remember acutely for what those minutes taught me.

My phone dinged. *Here we are,* her text said. *All alone in the back row. Soaking wet. Preacher trying like hell to save our souls.*

Sorry, I replied. *Will explain.* But I didn't know what I'd say except to agree that I should have told her sooner that we weren't coming. His wife would be forced to make excuses for him. I thought he was simply putting it off for as long as he could, that he'd rally at the last second and we'd get there, but I should have believed him from the beginning.

I said, "Looks like they went ahead to the funeral."

He pinched his bottom lip and stared toward the woods. His eyes grew wet and red. "I just couldn't go," he said. "I couldn't do it."

The rain continued at the same heavy pace for a long while, something of a miracle after so long a drought. I watched him watch it. For three seconds, his chin quivered, then stopped. His wet eyes grew smaller and redder, and they fixed themselves straight ahead now, as if he were peering deeper into the woods toward the back pew at his rain-soaked wife and daughter who were looking back at him, none too pleased, while Carl Smith sang, "If Teardrops Were Pennies." We sat still, saying nothing, and it was comfortable. The rain on the roof and in the yard joined the bands who accompanied all the singers who kept singing in succession, without interruption while we sat still and listened. Webb Pierce sang, "That's Me Without You," Faron Young sang, "I Miss You Already," Bobby Bare sang, "I'm 500 Miles Away From Home," Johnny Cash sang, "Give My Love to Rose," George Jones sang, "Life to Go," Tammy Wynette sang, "Apartment #9," Porter Wagoner sang, "Turn The Jukebox Up Louder," Dolly Parton sang, "Mule Skinner Blues," Stonewall Jackson sang, "Smoke Along the Track," Lefty Frizzell sang, "Heart's Highway," Ernest Tubb sang, "Lost Highway," and Hank Snow sang, "Headin' Down the Wrong Highway."

After the rain finally stopped and the cloud moved on and uncovered the sun, his wife and daughter pulled into the carport. They stayed in the car and stared at us. We were still sitting at the table, still in our swim trunks, still shirtless. They mouthed some words to each other we couldn't make out. The words weren't flattering—that was easy to tell. After another half-minute of staring at us, they got out and went inside, carrying shopping bags, saying nothing.

My father-in-law lifted his eyebrows at me. He said, "I couldn't go." And just like that he seemed to relax for the first time in three days, as if the rain and the sun that followed it—along with the safe return of his wife and daughter—had reminded him to breathe more deeply than he had in a long time.

Later, after they came out for an afternoon swim, after I lit the grill and filled the air with the scent of barbecued chicken and grilled vegetables while WSM (turned lower) went live from the Opry, and after I served it all up at the patio table where we ate all we wanted beneath the soft-blowing fan while the evening shadows closed over the yard toward the woods, and after we watched all the birds flock to his feeders again, after his cat finally came home to a refilled bowl, and after four grown deer strolled through the back yard and stopped to stare at us—after all of this, all was forgiven, and no one mentioned the funeral. We sat out there until it turned dark, and we spoke of nothing serious.

The next morning, a Sunday, my wife's parents waved from the driveway while we drove away in the hazy dawn light, both of them crying because of the distance we had to go and for the time that would elapse before we could return, and for the uncertainty of knowing whether all of us would survive that long. I waved out the window while I turned from the driveway and accelerated, and in the split second I gave myself to look back, it appeared to me that they were standing inside the woods, waving alongside all the other ghosts who were also waving.

Through the thirteen-hour drive, I kept seeing them. And I kept hearing my father-in-law's voice. I heard it while I crept through Nashville—closed to one lane because of an accident on Old Hickory Boulevard, and I kept hearing it while I stayed in the slow lane on I-65 and continued on I-24 across the western corner of Kentucky over the Ohio River and then up I-57 toward Champaign and followed a straight row through the ocean-sized cornfield of Illinois, where the landscape was punctuated every hundred miles by a half-dozen trees cloistered around a wrought-iron fence that held a family cemetery, then to I-74 toward Bloomington, then to I-39, and up, and up and then, just north of Normal, the big sky ahead of us quickly turned from grey to black and drooped down, the back end of the black sky hanging like a catcher's mitt. I drove toward it. I turned on my lights. No cars were coming southbound. In another second, heavy rain pounded the windshield. I turned my wipers on high and kept going. Cars ahead of me flashed their hazards. Drivers pulled to the shoulder. I kept going.

Ahead and to the right, a small patch of interstate held a puddle of bloody rain. The blood bounced around in the rain and turned a lighter shade of red. Just past this spot, a struck doe lay on her side, facing us. The doe lifted her head, long enough to look us in the eyes, then she lay it down again.

My wife covered her mouth with one hand. She said, "Oh dear God," which I first heard as "Oh *deer* God," which prompted a lips-closed laugh.

Lightning flashed eye-level in front of us, square in the center of the black catcher's mitt.

I drove slowly, following the flashing hazard lights of the car ahead of me, and still, above the sound of crashing rain, I heard my father-in-law's voice, so rich with music, bends, turns, dips, and doubling-backs. I wanted never to lose it. I imagined his voice—if we could keep it in our heads—would one day be a comfort to my wife and me when we got older and remained a long way away and had a hard time locating anything in the world that sounded authentic.

It took thirty minutes of going thirty miles per hour to get through the blackest part of the storm, where the heaviest rain pounded down on us. When we stopped to pay the toll near the Wisconsin state line, I'd turned my wipers on low, then just north of Beloit, I turned them off.

Close to dusk, we rolled across the beautiful part of southwestern Wisconsin known as the driftless region, which just that second resembled the rolling hills of middle Tennessee, where the people in my father-in-law's stories lived. They were people I'd never met, but I missed them. I missed watching his eyes watch them in the woods. I missed the shape his face took when he lost himself to laughter. I missed his wife and the way she doted over me, though I did not deserve it. I missed being outside with them on their patio that faced the pool and the woods on the far side of the yard where all the ghosts still gathered to gossip about the living.

I was far enough away to see them all more clearly now. And I felt old enough, suddenly, to see a version of myself as a much-older man who, with enough diligence, might resemble the man my father-in-law became: the kind of rare person who came to know himself honestly because of the time he devoted to sitting still and re-telling stories of how his time and place and the people in it shaped his life, while making no excuse for any of his choices.

My stomach made a violent noise that sounded like loneliness.

I grabbed my wife's hand.

"Here we are," I said.

"Here we are," she agreed. "Let's turn around."

I squeezed her hand. I said, "Ha-ha."

Acknowledgments

'm grateful to the editors of the following journals where some of these stories, with minor variations, first appeared: *Grist: A Journal for Writers*: ("Any Idiot Can Feel Pain,"); *Moon City Review*: ("Awful Pretty," and "What to do When Your Spouse is Burning,)"; *Passages North*: ("The Girl Who Drowned at School That Time,"); *Northwest Review*: ("Nothing Ruins a Good Story Like an Eyewitness"); *Saw Palm*: ("Clarissa Drives John Boy to the Jacksonville Airport"); *storySouth*: ("Penmanship," and "Chuck Langford Jr., Depressed Auctioneer, Takes Action"); *Willow Springs*: ("Last Words of the Holy Ghost,"); *Wisconsin Review:* ("Snell's Law").

I'm also grateful to Ben Sharony, who adapted "Last Words of the Holy Ghost," into a film that premiered at the 2012 Los Angeles Short Film Festival; it appeared at numerous other festivals and won awards at the Mexico International Film Festival and the Aquilar De Campoo Festival held in Leon, Spain. (More information at www.lastwordsfilm.com).

I am also eternally indebted to the following people for invaluable feedback, inspiration, and long-lasting support: Georgia Burgess-Erwin; John Cashion, Myrna and Clayton Jett, Alberta and Carlton D. Burgess, The Burgess Family Foundation for Prodigal Sons, Bob Powell, Joan and Joseph Bathanti, The Jean and Terry Beck Sanctuary for Wayward Southerners, Peggy

Cash, Tracy Daugherty, Patrick Gilsenan, Ehud Havazelet, Robin Hemley, Roxanne Newton, Jerry Saviano; Ben Sharony, Bim Staton, Robert Treu; Brian Turner, Bonnie Jo Stufflebeam, Karen DeVinney. I'm also appreciative for support from the North Carolina Arts Council, the Wisconsin Arts Council, the Wisconsin Writers Council, the University of Wisconsin-La Crosse committee on sabbaticals, UW-L Department of English colleagues, especially Susan Crutchfield. My deepest appreciation to Heather Jett, who read these stories and made them better, who lives with me and makes *me* better—my love, my life, my last words.

CPSIA information can be obtained at www.ICGtesting.com
Printed in the USA
LVOW07s1022240915

455470LV00002B/2/P